William H. Crosskill

Prince Edward Island

Garden Province of Canada - its history, interests, and resources with

information for tourists, etc

William H. Crosskill

Prince Edward Island

Garden Province of Canada - its history, interests, and resources with information for tourists, etc

ISBN/EAN: 9783337194796

Printed in Europe, USA, Canada, Australia, Japan

Cover: Foto ©Andreas Hilbeck / pixelio.de

More available books at **www.hansebooks.com**

QUEEN SQUARE GARDENS

Prince Edward Island

Garden Province of Canada

ITS HISTORY, INTERESTS, AND RESOURCES,

— WITH —

INFORMATION FOR TOURISTS, ETC.

W. H. CROSSKILL

OFFICIAL COURT STENOGRAPHER AND LEGISLATIVE LIBRARIAN

Published by the Provincial Government

CHARLOTTETOWN, P. E. ISLAND

MURLEY & GARNHUM, STEAM PRINTERS AND BOOKBINDERS

1899

"PRETTY ' " SUBJECTS FOR THE CAMERA AT EVERY TURN,"

"GOOD WAGGON ROADS ARE EVERYWHERE FOUND."

"INDENTED WITH BAYS AND LOVELY ARMS OF THE SEA."

CONTENTS.

Prince Edward Island

GARDEN PROVINCE OF CANADA

"O, it's a snug little island!
A right little, tight little island!"—Dibdin T.

GEOGRAPHICAL SITUATION

IN the great Bay of the Gulf of Saint Lawrence and separated from the Continent by the North-umberland Strait lies the beautiful Province of Prince Edward Island. It is situated between 46° and 47° 7′ North Latitude and 62° and 64° 27′ West Longitude, and is distant from New Brunswick at the nearest point 9 miles, from Nova Scotia 15 miles, and from Cape Breton 30 miles. The Island presents the form of an irregular crescent concaved towards the North, is 130 miles long, and from 2 to 34 miles wide, and contains an area of 2,133 square miles or 1,365,120 acres.

HISTORICAL SKETCH

Wrapped up in the mists of the cloudy past, the exact date of the discovery of Prince Edward Island is a matter of conjecture. A commonly accepted belief is that it was first sighted by John Cabot in 1497, who named it Saint John in honor of the day, June 24th, the anniversary of the death of Saint John the Baptist. Many writers contend that it was discovered by Cabot's son Sebastian in 1498, while other authorities state that to Champlain is to be accorded the honor of naming the Island and of planting thereon the *Fleur-de-lis.* Unfortunately no details of the early voyages have been preserved, and it is doubtful what navigator first viewed this Island.

The history of the Island of St. John may be divided into two distinct periods, namely, from its discovery until it passed into the hands of the British in 1763; and from that time to the present. The Island long remained in its primeval state. Neglected by the English Government, the French appropriated it as part of the discoveries made by Verrazzani, a native of Florence, in 1523. In 1534, Jacques Cartier, the intrepid mariner of St. Malo, made his first voyage to the new world. He first trod Canadian soil at Brest in Esquimaux Bay; thence touching at Newfoundland and the Magdalen Islands, he afterwards reached St. John's shore. There are extant several quaint descriptions of the country as he saw it, and from one, the " Relation Originale," we quote as follows :—

"All this land is low and the most beautiful it is possible to see, and full of beautiful trees and meadows; but in it we were not able to find a harbor, because it is a low land, very shallow and all ranged with sands. We went ashore in several places in our boats, and among others into a beautiful but very shallow river, where we saw boats of savages, which were crossing this river, which, on this account, we named the River of Boats.

That day we coasted along the said land nine or ten leagues, trying to find some harbor, which we could not; for as I have said before, it is a land low and shallow. We went ashore in four places to see the trees, which are of the very finest and sweet smelling, and found that they were cedars, pines, white elms, ashes, willows, and many others to us unknown. The lands where there are no woods are very beautiful, and all full of peason, white and red gooseberries, strawberries, blackberries, and wild grain like rye; it seems there to have been sown and ploughed. This is a land of the best temperature which it is possible to see, and of great heat, and there are many doves and thrushes and other birds; it only wants harbours."

In 1663, Isle St. Jean, with other Islands was granted by the Company of New France to Sieur Francois Doublet, a French Naval Captain, who, with others, established fishing stations; but it was not until the Peace of Utretch in 1713, which closed a fierce struggle between England and France, that the Island began to attract settlers.

About 1715 the permanent peopling commenced. The expulsion of the Acadians from Nova Scotia in 1755 considerably augmented the population. From 1713 to 1758 the colony was under the control of the French. Port la Joie (Charlottetown), Pinette and Crapaud appear to have been the earliest of the French settlements, but other places such as St Peter's, Rustico and Malpeque soon sprang up. But colonization was slow, for in 1728 the population was only 300, and in 1745 it did not exceed 1000 souls. At this time England and France were again at war, and the Island of St. John was captured by the New England forces; but it was afterwards restored to the French, by the Treaty of Aix-la-Chappelle. The fall of Louisburg caused several French families to remove from Cape Breton to Isle St. Jean. The great fortress was restored to France in 1748, but it again fell into the hands of the British in 1758 under the leadership of the gallant Wolfe. After the capture of Louisburg, the Island was seized by British Ships. At this time it was well stocked with horned cattle, and some corn was shipped annually to the Quebec market. And now followed the fall of Quebec, and by the Treaty of Fontainebleau in 1763, Cape Breton, the Island of St. John, and Acadia, were ceded to Great Britain, the two Islands named being placed under the Government of Nova Scotia. But the Acadians kept up a determined hostility, and during 1756 and 1757 assisted the Indians in committing depredations in Nova Scotia. Strong means were used to enforce their submission, and some were deported, while others returned to France rather than swear allegiance to England. In 1768 the islanders becoming dissatisfied with their connection with Nova Scotia, petitioned for a separate government agreeing to contribute a certain sum to meet their expenses. This request was complied with about two years afterwards, and Walter Patterson was appointed Governor. During the succeeding five years efforts were made to increase the population by the importation of Acadians, Highlanders and others; but it was not until July 7th, 1773, when Governor Patterson considered the Island sufficiently settled, that the General Assembly first met.

In the year 1775, two American schooners touched at Charlottetown, plundered the town, and carried off the Governor and other prominent citizens to the American headquarters; but Washington promptly dismissed the commanders, returned the prisoners, and restored the stolen property.

In 1780, the Legislature, on the suggestion of Governor Patterson, passed an Act changing the name of St. John to that of New Ireland, but this was disallowed. Its original name was retained until 1798, when, on account of the inconvenience arising from the fact that towns in two neighboring Colonies bore practically the same name, and also out of compliment to the Duke of Kent, at that time Commander of the Forces at Halifax, it was changed by an Act of the Colonial Legislature to Prince Edward Island. The Micmacs called it "Abegweit," "Home on the wave."

Prince Edward Island remained a separate Province from the 1st of May 1769, until July 1st, 1873, when it became a part of the Dominion of Canada. An agitation for the establishment of responsible Government started in 1834, resulted in this being granted in 1851, since which time, the Executive has been recognized as responsible to the Legislature. Some Acts of very great importance were afterwards passed, among others being those providing for the establishment of a uniform rate of postage, the assimilation of the currency, and free education; and in 1853 a measure was enacted which conferred universal suffrage on the people.

In 1766, a survey was made by Captain Samuel Holland, by which the Island was divided into 67 townships or lots, each containing about 20,000 acres. These grants were made by means of a lottery to a number of persons (principally officers of the Army and Navy) who were considered to have claims upon the British Government. Thus the whole Island, with the exception of some small reservations, passed from the Crown in one day. The results of this arrangement were very unsatisfactory. According to the terms of their grants, the grantees were to encourage the fisheries, pay a small sum as quit rents, and were to settle one person on every 200 acres of land within 10 years. Very few of the original grantees carried out the conditions, their only object being to convert the grants into ready cash as quickly as possible, and many of them sold their estates to parties in England. Notwithstanding these difficulties, however, shortly after the beginning of the present century, the country became populated with a race of hardy English, Scotch and Irish settlers, who formed separate communities and along with the French Colonists devoted themselves to agriculture and the fisheries.

Prior to Holland's survey, many plans were suggested for the settlement of the Colony. The most strenuous efforts were made by the Earl of Egmont, First Lord of the Admiralty, for a grant of the Island, and to hold the same in fee simple of the Crown. He proposed to settle it on a feudal plan, and that he himself should be Lord Paramount of the whole Island. His plans were set forth in a memorial to the King, and were backed up by several communications addressed to the Lords of Trades and Plantations, and signed by influential gentlemen distinguished for military and other services. The King referred the matter to the Board of Trade. In 1764 the Board reported against the adoption of Egmont's scheme, and his proposal was therefore rejected.

For over half a century, the Land Question was a source of trouble. Many attempts were made to settle it; but it was not until 1875, after the union of the Island with Canada, when a sum of $800,000 was placed at the service of the Island Government for the purchase of the proprietors' estates, that the difficulty was finally disposed of. This question has now become a thing of the past, absentee proprietorship has been abolished, and the Provincial Government has purchased the interests of the landlords with the object of making the farmers freeholders. The majority of the tenants have availed themselves of this immense advantage, and at the present time, only 50,000 acres remain unsold of the 843,981 acquired by the Government; and of this quantity, but 20,000 acres represent land held by parties who have not yet purchased. The remaining 30,000 acres may be regarded as the available uncultivated and vacant Government lands. These consist of forest lands of medium quality, the very best having, of course, been taken up by the tenants in the first instance, and their price averages about one dollar per acre. Parties purchasing are required to pay 30 per cent. down and the balance in two years.

SOME GENERAL CHARACTERISTICS

PRINCE EDWARD ISLAND is divided into three counties, Prince in the west, Queen's in the centre, and King's in the east. The coast line is exceedingly irregular being deeply indented with large bays and tidal estuaries, no part of the country being far distant from the sea. The principal high lands are a chain of hills which traverse the Island north and south between DeSable and New London Bay.

Geology

The oldest geological formations are represented by "beds of brown, gray and red sandstone and shale, with layers of coarse concretionary limestone and fossil plants." The desintegrated red sandstone forming the upper layers imparts a peculiar redness to the soil, a feature which always attracts the attention of strangers. The minerals are unimportant, neither coal, gypsum nor gold being found in any part. In Prince County are to be seen numbers of granite rocks lying in the fields many miles from the shore. These were evidently cast there by the ice in some bye-gone age.

CLIMATE

PRINCE EDWARD ISLAND has been justly termed the "Garden of British North America." The summer climate is perfect, and as Jacques Cartier described it "of the best temperature which it is possible to see." In June and July, the country is a paradise of bloom, verdure and foliage. Singularly free from extremes of heat and cold, there are not, as a rule, those sudden changes which one experiences on the mainland. Its summer heat is always tempered by the waters of the surrounding Gulf, and from every direction is borne on the breeze the life giving smell of the sea. The winter *per se* is not unpleasant, but the springs, owing to the prevalence of ice along the shores, are often backward. Of such brightness and beauty is the summer, however, that it amply compensates for the tedious spring. Navigation generally closes towards the end of December, and re-opens about the middle of April. The cold is neither so great in winter, nor the heat so intense in summer, as in the other Provinces of the Dominion, while the Island, sheltered from the Atlantic by the hills of Cape Breton and Newfoundland, is almost entirely free from fogs. The Autumn is a beautiful season.

The following table shows the mean highest, mean lowest, monthly mean, and average temperatures, &c., and the precipitation (in inches) at Charlottetown during the years 1895, 1896, 1897 and 1898.

1895

	Jan.	Feb.	March	Apr.	May	June	July	Aug.	Sept.	Oct.	Nov.	Dec.	Year
Mean highest	28.3	26.9	32.3	43.6	60.3	69.1	73.0	70.0	63.7	52.0	45.4	35.1	50.0
Mean lowest	13.7	9.3	16.7	29.8	43.5	52.0	58.9	57.7	50.3	39.1	33.0	23.9	35.7
Mean Range	14.6	17.6	15.6	13.8	16.8	17.1	14.1	12 3	13.4	12.9	12.4	11 2	14.3
Monthly mean	21.0	18.1	24.5	36.7	51.9	60.6	65.9	63.8	57.0	45.5	39.3	29.5	42 8
Warmest day	43.1	35.5	43.1	57.0	78.4	81.4	82.1	79.3	75.4	64.0	59.3	51.0	
Coldest day	-7.0	-14.8	4.0	16.0	28.2	40.0	50.5	48.8	37.7	28.1	21.0	11.5	
Rain	.91		.68	1.08	3.36	.53	3.46	6.54	3.61	2.74	5.92	2.05	30.88
Snow ⎰ Rain,	26.50	41.50	11.60	10.50								3.90	4.80	98.80
Total ⎱ melted Snow	3.56	4.15	1.84	2.13	3.36	.53	3.46	6.54	3.61	2.74	6.31	2 53	40.76

Mean for the year   3.40

1896

	Jan.	Feb.	March	Apr.	May	June	July	Aug.	Sept.	Oct.	Nov.	Dec.	Year
Mean highest	25.5	25.8	34.6	42.2	56.1	64 5	72.9	70.0	63.7	53.5	42.8	29.8	48.5
Mean lowest	12.7	10.6	21.1	28.4	38 2	49.4	58.3	57.0	50 0	42.6	29.6	16.2	34.5
Mean range	12.8	15.2	13.5	13.8	17.9	15.1	14.6	13.0	13.7	10.9	13.2	13 6	14.0
Monthly mean	19.1	18 2	27.9	35.3	47.1	56.9	65.6	63.5	56 9	48.0	36.2	23.0	41.5
Warmest day	39.4	41.9	49.1	61.7	71.0	76 6	81.6	77.1	79.4	66.8	55.0	43.9	
Coldest day	-12.0	-9.2	8.0	22.3	28.7	40.3	49.5	48.5	40.7	32.1	11.3	0.0	
Rain	.12	.28	2.73	.48	1.25	3.78	4.70	1.80	3 20	10.38	2.13	1 64	32.49
Snow ⎰ Rain,	16.70	12.00	17.30	1.60							4 20	5.50	57 30
Total ⎱ melted Snow	1.79	1.48	4.46	.64	1.25	3.78	4.70	1.80	3.20	10.38	2.55	2.19	38 22

Mean for the year   3.19

1897

	Jan.	Feb.	March	Apr.	May	June	July	Aug.	Sept.	Oct.	Nov.	Dec.	Year
Mean highest	26.6	24.6	33.1	45.6	56.2	62.4	72.5	71.0	62.2	53.2	40.7	32.4	48.4
Mean lowest	11.0	8.3	18.3	30.3	41.5	48.3	58.5	57.9	48.9	39.6	29.4	21.5	34.5
Mean range	15.6	16.3	14.8	15.3	14.7	14.1	14.0	13.1	13.3	13.6	11.3	10.9	13.9
Monthly mean	18.8	16.5	25.7	37.9	48.8	55 3	65 5	64.4	55.5	46.4	35 0	26.9	41.4
Warmest day	51.7	36.6	45.2	65.0	72.0	74.1	85 1	76 8	79.0	64.7	53.0	52 0	
Coldest day	-16.5	-9.5	-11.0	6.2	29.8	40.2	46.5	52 0	39.7	21.1	14 5	2.5	
Rain	1.26		2.64	2 72	3 25	3.65	4 52	3 10	3 29	1.84	5 40	1.82	33.49
Snow ⎰ Rain,	13.00	16.20	13.10	5.40							2.20	6.50	56.40
Total ⎱ melted Snow	2.56	1.62	3.95	3.26	3.25	3.65	4.52	3.10	3.29	1 84	5.62	2.47	39.13

Mean for the year   3.26

1898

	Jan.	Feb.	March	Apr.	May	June	July	Aug.	Sept.	Oct.	Nov.	Dec.	Year
Mean highest	22.4	30.3	37.5	43.3	56.3	64.3	71 6	71.5	63.6	54.2	45.8	33 2	49.5
Mean lowest	6.0	17.7	25.9	31.5	40.8	52.0	59.0	61.4	51.7	42 4	35.5	19.8	37.0
Mean range	16.4	12.6	11.6	11.8	15.5	12 3	12.6	10 1	11.9	11.8	10.3	13 4	12.5
Monthly mean	14.2	24.0	31.7	37 4	48.5	58.1	65.3	66 5	57.6	48.3	40.6	26.5	43.2
Warmest day	39.5	39.7	49.5	54.2	73.8	73.0	83 3	77.3	77.0	76.8	58.7	45.2	
Coldest day	-15.6	-6 2	15.7	24.6	28 8	44.8	48.6	53.1	34.5	32.0	23.2	-7.9	
Rain	1.48	.22	1.02	4.49	2.36	2.76	3.35	4.54	2.50	5.23	5.21	1.36	34.52
Snow ⎰ Rain,	27.40	6.60	10.70	2.50							4.50	13.70	65.40
Total ⎱ melted Snow	4.22	.88	2.09	4.74	2.36	2.76	3.35	4.54	2 50	5.23	5.66	2.73	41.06

Mean for the year   3.42

The following table gives the average summer and yearly temperature, derived from 10 years' observations, at three points in the Island, with the latitude, longitude and height above the sea.—

STATION	Latitude	Longitude	Elevation above sea	Mean Temperature	
	° ′	° ′ ″	feet	Summer °	Year °
Charlottetown	46 14	63.10 22	38	62.2	40 7
Georgetown	46.11	62.35	100	61.2	40.9
Alberton	46.48	64. 2	20	61.2	39 2

SCENERY

EEN from the water, the appearance of this wave-girt Province is very attractive. The country is picturesque and pleasing, but it is devoid of the romantic boldness which characterizes the north shore of the Gulf. Although generally level, in some parts it is beautifully undulating. To use the oft-quoted yet appropriate lines of the late Hunter Duvar, a gifted Island writer:

"A long low line of beach, with crest of trees,
With openings of rich verdure, emerald-hued,
* * * And this fair land is Epaygooyat called,
An Isle of golden grain and healthful clime,
With vast fish-teeming waters, ocean-walled,
The smallest Province of the Maritime."

The scenery is of pastoral simplicity, and resembles that of England, and the country is thickly dotted with comfortable homesteads. The Island is much indented with bays and lovely arms of the sea, and the peculiar greenness of its fields and meadows rivals in beauty that of the Emerald Isle itself. Facing the Gulf are fifty miles of white sand dunes, washed by the cool waters of the sea, and forming one of the finest bathing grounds in the world. The average temperature of the water is about 65 degrees.

" DOTTED WITH COMFORTABLE HOMESTEADS "

"FIFTY MILES OF WHITE SAND DUNES"

ITS POPULATION

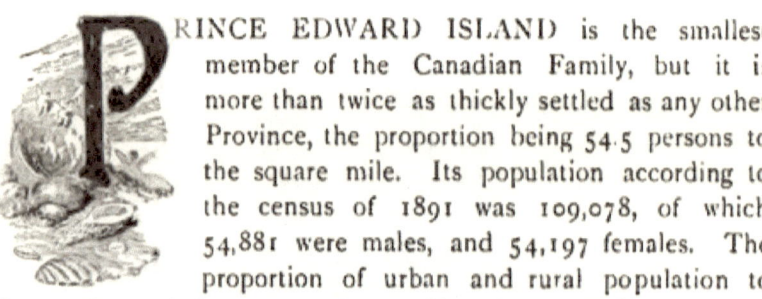

RINCE EDWARD ISLAND is the smallest member of the Canadian Family, but it is more than twice as thickly settled as any other Province, the proportion being 54.5 persons to the square mile. Its population according to the census of 1891 was 109,078, of which 54,881 were males, and 54,197 females. The proportion of urban and rural population to the total population was: urban 13% and rural 87%.

The Scotch muster about 49,000, the Irish 25,000, the English 21,000, and the French about 12,000. The Roman Catholics number 47,837, the Presbyterians 32,988, the Methodists 13,596, Church of England 6,646, and the Baptists 6,265. Churches prettily situated are numerous, and the Roman Catholic body possesses brick edifices on commanding sites at Tignish, Fort Augustus, Vernon River, St. Peters' Bay, Souris and elsewhere. In 1891 there were 266 churches, of which 85 were Presbyterian, 68 were Methodist, 43 Roman Catholic, 42 Baptist, 21 Church of England, and 7 miscellaneous. The number of Clergymen was 122. The inhabitants are largely engaged in agriculture; but some attention is devoted to the fisheries and to the breeding of stock. As will be seen from the above, the population is of mixed origin, a considerable proportion being emigrants from Great Britain and Ireland, and the remainder, descendants of the settlers placed there by the original grantees of the lots, and of the French who escaped deportation at the hands of the English. Up to within comparatively recent times the French lived quite apart and kept up the traditions and customs of the past.

The Gaelic tongue is still spoken in many localities. But the spread of education, improved travelling facilities, and other influences are fast eradicating these racial distinctions. The progressive increase of population is shown by the following :—

In 1728 the population numbered			300
1749	"	"	1,000
1765	"	"	1,400
1784	"	"	3,000
1806	"	"	9,676
1822	"	"	24,600
1825	"	"	28 600
1827	"	"	23,266
1833	"	"	32,292
1841	"	"	47,034
1850	"	"	55,000
1861	"	"	80,552
1871	"	"	94,021
1881	"	"	108,891
1891	"	"	109,078

THE INDIANS OF P. E. ISLAND

THE Indians are of the Micmac tribe a branch of the great Algonquin race. There are 81 men, 79 women, and 143 children, a total of 303. In 1871 they numbered 323, and in 1881, 281. There are two Reserves. One is situated on Lennox Island, in Richmond Bay and contains 1,320 acres. The other is at Morell, Lot 40, in King's County. On the Lennox Island Reserve, is a school attended by 28 children, and a fine church. All the members of this band are Roman Catholic. These

Indians are quiet and inoffensive and for the most part temperate. Their principal occupations are farming, fishing and the manufacture of Indian wares. They had in 1897, 130 acres of land cultivated, 9 acres of newly broken land, and 120 farming implements. They raised 78 horses, cattle, sheep, etc., 1,151 bushels of grain, 695 bushels of potatoes and roots, 78 tons of hay. The value of Fish, Furs and other industries amounted to $9,545. The present Chief is John Sark.

CHIEF JOHN SARK

How P. E. Island is Governed

IN addition to the Central Government at Ottawa, there exists in Prince Edward Island as in the other Provinces of the Dominion, a Local Legislature for the control of all matters of Provincial importance. This Government is vested in the Lieutenant Governor appointed for 5 years by the Federal Administration, and whose salary is $7,000 per annum, an Executive Council of 9 members who have seats in the Legislature and who are responsible to the same, and a Legislative Assembly elected by the people. The Sessional indemnity is $160, with an allowance for mileage, stationery, etc.

The Executive Council is composed as follows:—

> Premier,
> Attorney General,
> Provincial Secretary-Treasurer and Commissioner of
>   Crown and Public Lands,
> Commissioner of Public Works,
> And Five Ministers without portfolio.

Prior to 1893, there were two branches of the Legislature, one called the Legislative Council, representing the property holders, and the other the House of Assembly. The Legislative Council consisted of 13 members elected from certain large constituencies. The House of Assembly consisted of 30 Members elected from smaller constituencies. The Legislative Councillors were elected by voters who owned freehold or leasehold property to the value of $325. The Members of the House of Assembly were elected practically by manhood suffrage.

The present Legislative Assembly is the result of the amalgamation of these two Houses which took place in 1893. It consists of 30 Members—15 Councillors elected by one set of electors, and 15 Assemblymen elected by two sets of electors, one of each being returned by the 15 districts into which the Island is divided. These sit side by side and have exactly the same powers. The protection supposed to be given to property holders by the Legislative Council still exists. There is no property qualification for either Councillors or Assemblymen. For the electors of Councillors the qualifications are British citizenship, full age of 21 years or upwards, and the ownership of property to the value of $325. The qualifications for the electors of Assemblymen in addition to citizenship and full age, are ownership or occupancy of real estate of the yearly value of $6 for 6 months before teste of writ, or a residence of 12 months, and the performance of statute labor on the public roads, or in lieu thereof, the payment of 75 cents commutation money. The number of voters is 25,245.

The duration of the Assembly is four years unless sooner dissolved, and the sessions are held annually in March or April.

The Legislature expends money for Provincial Legislation, Administration of Justice (except Judges' salaries), Education, Public Works, such as Wharfs (being of Provincial as distinguished from Dominion or Federal importance), Ferries, Roads, Bridges, etc. It maintains offices for the Registration of Deeds, Mortgages, Wills, Judgments, etc., and pays for Poor House Maintenance, Inspectors of Licenses, Hospital for Insane, Coroners' Inquests, Boards of Health, Dairy Associations, etc.

For educational purposes, the Province is divided into School Districts, each of which has authority to spend moneys for school buildings, running expenses, and supplements for teachers' salaries.

The City of Charlottetown (which is incorporated) expends money for general civic purposes, such as streets, sewers, water works, fire prevention, city buildings, lighting streets, etc., and the towns of Summerside and Georgetown (the latter to a very limited extent) have somewhat similar powers.

Prince Edward Island has not yet adopted the municipal system, and the expenditure of the Provincial Revenue is authorized directly by the Legislature.

The principal sources of revenue are the Dominion Subsidy,

Direct Taxation of Land, Income Tax, Succession Duties, Commercial Travellers', Peddlers', Vendors' and Marriage Licenses, Incorporated Companies' Tax, Public Lands, Prothonotary, Registry, Provincial Secretary Office Fees and County Court Fees.

The following table shows the Receipts and Expenditures of the Province for 1898.

RECEIPTS

Dominion Subsidy	$181,952.95
Public Lands	14,273.88
Commercial Travellers' Licenses	4,860.00
Incorporated Companies	4,275.00
Ferries	5,740.00
Prothonotary's Offices	2,029.31
Registry Offices	4,745.50
County Courts	1,154.77
Provincial Land Tax	30,084.48
Income Tax	5,556.74
Debentures sold	18,094.77
Various other sources of Revenue	3,415.58
	$276,182.98

EXPENDITURES

Administration of Justice	$ 17,022.68
Civil Government	13,710.62
Education	129,817.81
Ferries	19,749.35
Legislation	7,789.43
Roads	14,712.40
Bridges	15,137.42
Hospital for Insane	19,735.05
Poor Asylum and Charities	6,933.49
Interest	18,558.80
Wharves	3,376.29
Miscellaneous Public Works	15,672.41
Debenture Sinking Fund	2,775.00
Various other Expenditures	7,966.00
	$292,956.75
Capital Expenditure	8,743.00
	$301,699.75

STATEMENT showing the Revenues and Expenditures of the Province of Prince Edward Island for the years 1868 to 1898.

YEAR	RECEIPTS	EXPENDITURES
1868	$270,559	$299,867
1869	288,722	312,653
1870	302,855	343,892
1871	385,014	406,236
1872	395,473	506,666
† 1873	* 484,979	* 401,662
1874	403,013	442,767
1875	306,597	395,277
1876	524,144	353,226
1877	326,274	331,632
1878	312,684	334,133
1879	288,062	313,845
1880	269,603	257,309
1881	275,380	261,276
1882	233,465	257,228
1883	228,169	270,477
1884	280,271	279,545
1885	248,222	266,318
1886	233,978	304,467
1887	241,637	288,052
1888	254,209	279 939
1889	‡ 434,635	263,605
1890	224,882	305,799
1891	274,047	304,486
1892	245,652	259,012
1893	217,473	294,201
1894	282,468	280,596
1895	277,314	310,177
1896	273,496	287,631
1897	272,550	310,752
1898	276,183	301.700

* 11 months only.

† NOTE —Prior to and including 1872 the financial year closed at the 31st January. In 1873 the present system of closing the accounts at the 31st December came into force.

‡ Including $200,000 drawn from capital at Ottawa.

TAXATION

Taxation outside of the municipalities of Charlottetown and Summerside, is very moderate, and is applied to the maintenance of the Provincial Government.

LAND TAX

The present Land Tax system was introduced in 1894, and the amount paid ranged from 1 to 6 cents per acre according to the value. In 1897 the Act was amended and a percentage tax at the rate of one-fifth of one per cent. on the value of the property, or 20 cents on $100, was adopted. The owner makes a declaration before the Deputy Receiver of Taxes, of the cash market value of the land with the appurtenances, and on this the percentage is paid. The value of the land includes the value of the buildings thereon ; but no improvements are embraced after the first year. This tax is collected either from the owner, tenant or occupier, and the land, as well as goods and chattels, is liable. In case of undervaluation provision is made for proceedings at the expense of the owner to ascertain the correct value. This, however, has rarely to be resorted to. Cemeteries and Church Yards are exempt.

INCOME TAX

The assessable income of every person receiving wages or salary for any employment or income from his or her own actual manual labor is calculated upon the amount over $350. Every other person is taxed on the full amount of his or her income. The sum to be paid is left to the voluntary declaration of the individual. Non-residents of the Province receiving an income from money invested or property situated therein, are liable. The present rate is one per cent.

Speakers House of Assembly

R. Stewart,	1773	A. Fletcher,	1790
John Budd,	1776	J. Robinson,	1790
D. Higgins,	1779	J. Stewart,	1795
W. Berry,	1780	J. Curtis,	1801
A. Fletcher,	1785	R. Hodgson,	1806
P. Callbeck,	1788	R. Brecken,	1812

Speakers House of Assembly--(Continued)

J. Curtis,	1813	Joseph Wightman,	1867
Angus Macaulay, M. D.,	1818	John Yeo,	1871
John Stewart,	1825	Stanislaus Perry,	1873
W. Macneill,	1831	Cornelius Howat,	1874
George Dalrymple,	1835	Henry Beer,	1877
William Cooper,	1839	John A. McDonald,	1883
Joseph Pope,	1843	Patrick Blake,	1890
Alexander Rae,	1850	Bernard D. McLellan,	1891
John Jardine,	1854		
Edward Thornton,	1854	**Legislative Assembly**	
Donald Montgomery,	1859	James H. Cummiskey,	1894

Presidents Legislative Council

John Duport,	1773	S. G. W. Archibald,	1825
P. Callbeck,	1774	George Wright,	1827
J. R. Spence,	1776	E. J. Jarvis,	1829
P. Stewart,	1779	T. H. Haviland,	1839
T. DesBrisay,	1780	Robert Hodgson,	1840
P. Callbeck,	1786	Donald McDonald,	1853
T. DesBrisay,	1788	Charles Young, L. L. D.,	1854
P. Stewart,	1790	Donald Montgomery,	1863
R. Thorp,	1802	Herbert Bell,	1874
T. DesBrisay,	1805	Joseph Wightman,	1876
C. Colclough,	1808	John Balderston,	1877
T. Tremlett,	1813	Thomas Walker Dodd,	1887
C. Worrell,	1825	Benjamin Rogers,	1891

Provincial Premiers

George Coles, 1851, Lib.

John Holl, Feby., 1854, Con.

George Coles, July, 1855, Lib.

Edward Palmer, April, 1859. Con.

John H. Gray, 1863, Con.

James Colledge Pope, 1865, Con

George Coles, 1867, Lib.

Joseph Hensley, 1869, Lib.

Robert P. Haythorne, 1870, Lib.

J. C. Pope, Sept., 1870, Lib.-Con.

Provincial Premiers —(Continued)

Robert P. Haythorne, April 1872, Lib.-Con.

J. C. Pope, April 18, 1873 to Sept. 23, 1873, Lib.-Con.

Lemuel C. Owen, Sept. 23, 1873 to Sept. 4, 1876, Lib.-Con.

Louis Henry Davies, Sept. 6, 1876 to March 7, 1879, Coalition

William W. Sullivan, March 11, 1879 to Nov. 12, 1889, Lib.-Con.

Neil McLeod, Nov. 12, 1889 to April 21, 1891, Lib.-Con.

Frederick Peters, April 21, 1891 to Oct. 26, 1897, Lib

Alex. Bannerman Warburton, Oct. 27, 1897 to Aug. 1, 1898, Lib.

Donald Farquharson, August, 1, 1898, Lib.

Attorneys General

Philip Callbeck,	September 19, 1770
Joseph Aplin,	
John Wentworth,	June, 3. 1780
Peter Macgowan,	September 15, 1800
Charles Stewart,	November 4, 1811
Wm. Johnstone,	January 15, 1813
Robert Hodgson,	May 18, 1829
Charles Young,	May 29, 1851
Joseph Hensley,	May 2, 1853
Charles Young,	June 29, 1858
Frederick Brecken,	April 11, 1859
Edward Palmer,	January 28, 1863
Joseph Hensley,	March 14, 1867
Dennis O'M. Reddin,	(Solicitor General,) 1869
Frederick Brecken,	September 10, 1870
Edward Palmer,	April 18, 1873
L. H. Davies,	September 6, 1876
W. W. Sullivan,	March 11, 1878
Neil McLeod,	November 21, 1889
Frederick Peters,	April 21, 1891
H. C. Macdonald,	October 27, 1897

THE JUDICIARY

The Judiciary consists of a Supreme Court with one Chief Justice and two assistant Judges (the Master of the Rolls and the Vice-Chancellor), which Court meets in Charlottetown, Summerside and Georgetown; a Court of Chancery of which the Lieutenant Governor was formerly Chancellor, and the judicial powers of which are exercised by the Master of the Rolls and the Vice Chancellor ; a Court of Marriage and Divorce, instituted in 1836, of which the Lieutenant Governor and Members of the Executive Council are Judges (this exists as yet but in name); a Court of Vice-Admiralty with one Judge (the Chief Justice); a Court of Probate and Wills with one Judge ; three County Courts with one Judge for each ; a City Court in Charlottetown with one Judge ; and Stipendiary Magistrates and Justices of the Peace.

Prince Edward Island has authority to make its own civil laws, but in all criminal cases the form employed by the Courts is the Criminal Law of the Dominion.

Chief Justices

	Appointed
John Duport,	September 19, 1770
Peter Stewart,	June 23, 1776
Thomas Cochrane,	October 24, 1801
Robert Thorpe,	November 10, 1802
Casar Colclough,	May 1, 1807
Thomas Tremlett,	April 6, 1813
S. G. W. Archibald,	August 7, 1824
E. J. Jarvis,	August 30, 1828
Sir Robert Hodgson,	April 2, 1853
Edward Palmer,	July 7, 1874
William Wilfred Sullivan,	November 12, 1889

FEDERAL REPRESENTATION

The Province is represented in the Dominion Parliament by four Senators, and by five Members in the House of Commons.

THE MILITIA

In Military affairs the Island is the Twelfth District of Canada. The established strength of the active force by arms is composed of five companies of Garrison Artillery, one double company of Engineers, and eight companies of Infantry, a total of 60 officers and 646 non-commissioned officers and men.

GOVERNORS

The Governors of Prince Edward Island have been :—

In connection with Nova Scotia

Montague Wilmot,	1763 to 1766
Lord William Campbell,	1766 to 1770

As a separate Province

Walter Patterson,	1770 to May 1774
P. Callbeck, (Administrator)	Aug., 1775 to July 31, 1779
Thos. Des Brisay, (Administrator)	July 31, 1779 to July 6, 1786
Lieut.-General Edmund Fanning,	July 6, 1786
Col. J. F. W. Des Barres,	July, 1805
W. Townshend, (Administrator)	Oct. 21, 1812 to July 13. 1813
Charles Douglas Smith,	July 13, 1813
George Wright, (Administrator)	1825 to 1826
Col. John Ready,	Oct. 24, 1825
Sir Aretas W. Young,	Sept. 27, 1831 to Dec. 1. 1835
George Wright, (Administrator)	May 18, 1834 to Sept. 29, 1834
George Wright, (Administrator)	Dec. 2, 1835 to Aug. 30, 1836
Sir John Harvey,	Aug. 30, 1836 to 1837
George Wright, (Administrator)	1837
Sir Charles Augustus Fitzroy	June 25, 1837 to Nov. 2, 1841
George Wright, (Administrator)	Nov. 2, 1841 to Nov. 13, 1841
Sir Henry Vere Huntley,	Nov. 13, 1841 to Nov. 1, 1847
Ambrose Lane, (Administrator)	July 25, 1847 to Oct. 7, 1847
Sir Donald Campbell,	Dec. 9, 1847 to Oct. 10, 1850
Ambrose Lane, (Administrator)	Oct. 10, 1850 to Mar. 10, 1851
Sir Alexander Bannerman,	March 10, 1851
Sir Dominick Daly,	July 12, 1854
Charles Young, (Administrator)	May 26, 1859 to June 7, 1859
George Dundas,	June 8, 1859 to Oct. 22, 1868
Sir R. Hodgson, (Administrator)	1865
Sir R. Hodgson, (Administrator)	Oct. 22, 1868 to Oct 6, 1870
W. C. F. Robinson,	Oct. 7, 1870 to Nov. 15, 1873
Sir R. Hodgson, (Administrator)	July 30, 1873 to July 18, 1874
Sir Robert Hodgson	July 18, 1874 to July 18, 1879
T. H. Haviland, Q. C.,	July 19, 1879 to Aug. 1, 1884
Andrew A. MacDonald,	Aug. 1, 1884 to Sept. 4, 1889

Governors—(Continued)

J. S. Carvell,	Sept. 5, 1889 to Feb. 14, 1894
Wm. W. Sullivan, (Administrator)	Feb. 4, 1893 to May 31, 1893
Wm. W. Sullivan, (Administrator)	Feb. 14, 1894 to Feb 21, 1894
George W. Howlan,	Feb. 24. 1894 to June 1, 1899
Peter A. McIntyre,	June 1. 1899,

General Assemblies since 1873

No of General Assemblies	Sessions	Date of		
		Opening	Prorogation	Dissolution
1st	1st	March 4, 1874	April 28, 1874	
	2nd	" 18, 1875	" 27, 1875	July 1, 1876
	3rd	" 16, 1876	" 29, 1876	
2nd	1st	" 15, 1877	" 18, 1877	
	2nd	" 14, 1878	" 18, 1878	March 12, 1879
	3rd	Feb. 27, 1879	Mar. 11, 1879	
3rd	1st	April 24. 1879	June 7, 1879	
	2nd	March 4, 1880	April 26, 1880	
	3rd	" 1, 1881	" 5, 1881	April 15, 1882
	4th	" 8, 1882	" 8, 1882	
4th	1st	" 20, 1883	" 27, 1883	
	2nd	" 6, 1884	" 17, 1884	June 5, 1886
	3rd	" 11, 1885	" 11, 1885	
	4th	April 8, 1886	May 14, 1886	
5th	1st	Mar. 29, 1887	May 7, 1887	
	2nd	Mar. 22, 1888	April 28, 1888	Jan. 7, 1890
	3rd	Mar. 14, 1889	" 17, 1889	
6th	1st	Mar. 27, 1890	May 7, 1890	
	2nd	Apr. 23, 1891*	July 15, 1891	Nov. 18, 1893
	3rd	Mar. 23, 1892	May 5, 1892	
	4th	March 8, 1893	April 20, 1893	
7th	1st	" 28, 1894	May 9, 1894	
	2nd	" 21, 1895	April 19, 1895	June 25, 1897
	3rd	" 24, 1896	" 30, 1896	
	4th	" 30, 1897	May 1, 1897	
8th	1st	April 5, 1898	May 14, 1898	
	2nd	April 17, 1899	May 19, 1899	

* Adjourned to the 16th June.

The New Prince of Wales College

PRINCE EDWARD ISLAND'S EDUCATIONAL SYSTEM

RINCE EDWARD ISLAND possesses an excellent educational system, which is under the control of a Board composed of the Chief Superintendent of Education, the Principal of the Prince of Wales College and Normal School, and the Members of the Executive Council. There are three Inspectors, one for each County, and also an Inspector of French Schools. The Island is divided into school districts, and in each of these there are elected annually by the ratepayers, three trustees who serve for a term of three years, one retiring every year. Schools are supported partly by government grants and partly by district assessments. The school age is between the years of 5 and 16. Attendance between 8 and 13 is compulsory, but it has never been enforced. The school system is free. Schools are divided into three classes, primary, advanced and high. In the country districts the school houses are rarely more than three miles apart, and in the majority of cases, there is but one teacher for each. There are, however, a number of graded schools.

Prior to 1852, when the Free School system was introduced, the schools were mainly supported by voluntary subscription and with such local assistance as could be had. Before that year, there existed some good private schools, and one Central Academy for the higher branches of knowledge, but there was no definite school system. Since 1877, the year in which the Public Schools' Act was passed, many improvements have been introduced into the educational system.

The average salary paid first-class male teachers is $440, female teachers $332; second-class male teachers $254, female teachers $221; third-class male teachers $197, and female teachers $150.

Teachers are paid from the Provincial Treasury, but such salaries may be supplemented by local assessment. Those employed previous to 1896 are, after a service of five years, entitled to a small bonus.

The total number of teachers in 1898 was 581; of school districts 470; and of schools 468. The number of pupils was 21,852, and the average daily attendance was 13,377. The total expenditure for education by the Provincial Government was $129,817.81.

The Teaching Staff

Candidates for teachers must hold certificates from the Board of Education, based on examination, and on at least five months' attendance at the Normal School. These certificates are first, second and third-class.

The number of teachers employed according to class in the year 1898 was as follows :—

	Class I	Class II	Class III
Male Teachers	71	181	68
Female Teachers	30	143	88
Total	101	324	156

The following statement shows the educational growth from the year 1833.

YEAR	NO. OF SCHOOLS	NO. OF PUPILS
1833	74	2,176
1837	51	1,649
1841	121	4,356
1847	125	5,000
1851	135	5,366
1856	268	11,000
1861	302	12,102
1870	372	15,000
1871	381	15,795
1874	403	18,233
1878	465	19,240
1881	486	21,601
1887	437	22,460
1891	531	22,138
1897	467	21,845
1898	468	21,852

The dates of the principal Educational events are :—

1821. National School opened.
1825. First Education Act passed.

1830. First Board of Education appointed

1836. Central Academy opened.

1837. First Official Inspector of Schools appointed.

1838. First Teachers' Association formed.

1852. Free Education Act passed.

1855. St. Dunstan's College opened.

1856. Provincial Normal School established.

1860. Prince of Wales College established.

1877. Public Schools' Act passed, and a Department of Education instituted.

1879. Prince of Wales College and Provincial Normal School amalgamated, and Ladies admitted to the College.

1885. Arbor Day established for the Schools.

1887. Provincial Teachers' Association founded.

1896. Provincial Teachers' Association incorporated.

1899. New Prince of Wales College erected.

The Provincial Teachers' Association meeting annually, and the Charlottetown Teachers' Institute which meets fortnightly during the winter, are flourishing organizations, doing much to promote the cause of education.

The following table is a summary of the Educational statistics of the Province from 1885 to 1898 :—

Year	No. of School Departments in operation	No. of Teachers	Pupils Enrolled	Average Attendance	Percentage of Attendance	EXPENDITURE		
						Govern't	School Board	Total
1885	507	494	21,983	12,166	55,34	109,317	36,282	145,599
1886	509	498	22,414	12,612	56,27	111,992	36,787	148,779
1887	510	505	22,460	12,325	54,87	110,485	36,294	146,779
1888	512	509	22,478	12,248	54,49	108,846	38,609	117,455
1889	523	518	23,045	13,159	57,10	108,092	37,810	145,902
1890	529	529	22,530	12,490	55,43	113,626	37,610	151,236
1891	531	531	22,330	12,898	57,75	111,154	35,629	147,783
1892	538	538	22,169	12,986	58,58	114,570	36,542	151,112
1893	543	543	22,292	12,960	58,13	118,106	34,592	152,698
1894	556	553	22,221	12,849	58,00	122,077	37,854	159,937
1895	561	559	22,250	13,254	59,56	121,781	39,426	161,201
1896	569	569	22,138	13,412	60,58	124,084	34,809	158,893
1897	579	579	21,845	12,978	59,44	128,663	32,781	161,444
1898	581	581	21,852	13,377	61,58	129,818	33,135	162,953

The number of Pupils in the Indian Schools of Prince Edward Island in the years 1892 to 1897 was:—

1892	·	43
1893	- -	43
1894	·	33
1895	- -	31
1896	·	33
1897	- -	28

Colleges, etc.

The Prince of Wales College and Normal School is undenominational. It is situated in Charlottetown and has a staff of a Principal and four Professors. In connection with the College is a Model School with two teachers. This is the only Government Educational Institution where fees are charged, the rates being $10 for the session (year) for students resident in the City of Charlottetown, and $5 per annum for country pupils. Graduating Diplomas were first conferred in 1885, and are of three grades—Honour, First-class Ordinary and Second-class Ordinary. These Diplomas are accepted by the Faculty of Pine Hill Presbyterian Theological College, Halifax, as sufficient in certain subjects for admission to that Institution, and by all the Faculties in McGill University in the place of the entrance examinations.

St. Dunstan's Roman Catholic College (annexed to Laval University, Quebec) is located in the suburbs of Charlottetown, and is under the direction of the Bishop of the Diocese. At this Institution the fees are:—For boarders per term of 5 months $53 ; day scholars per annum $12 ; day scholars who follow the course in Philosophy and in Sciences, per annum $25. This College confers degrees, and many students attend from abroad. The Roman Catholic Church also possesses two Convent Schools in Charlottetown, ands everal others in different parts of the Island, where boarders are received.

At St. Peter's School for boys and girls, which is connected with the Church of England of that name in Charlottetown, pupils are prepared for matriculation into King's College, Windsor, N. S. The fees are $24 per annum for boys, and $15 for girls.

Scholarships, etc.

Examinations for scholarships in connection with the Prince of Wales College and Normal School are held biennially. These scholarships are eight in number. Six of the annual value of $80 are held for two years, and entitle the possessors to exemption from fees. Two are assigned to each of the three counties, and the competition is restricted to pupils who reside in the particular county. The two remaining scholarships, which scuure for the successful candidates immunity from fees, but confer no endowment, are reserved for pupils from schools in the City of Charlottetown. The examination for these scholarships is the same as that designated the Junior Entrance Examination.

There are no scholarships in connection with St. Dunstan's College. The "Connolly Bequest" provides for the education of boys of Irish parentage. These young men can be sent by the Trustees of the Fund to any Institution, but they generally enter St. Dunstan's to prepare for the Universities.

The "Daniel Hodgson Scholarship," entitling the holder to a three years' course, and worth $150 per annum, is open for competition to intending students for King's College, Windsor, N. S., or Laval University, Quebec, alternately.

The following medals are awarded at the Prince of Wales College :—

The Anderson Gold Medal to the most distinguished Student ; the Governor General's Silver Medal to the best student in Mathematics ; the Governor General's Bronze Medal to the best student-teacher in the department of School Management ; and the Vice-Chancellor's Medal to the best student in English.

His Excellency the Governor General also awards Bronze Medals annually to the student having the highest standing in the three Public Schools of Charlottetown, and in the High Schools at Summerside, Alberton, Tignish, Souris and Georgetown.

THE RESOURCES OF THE GARDEN PROVINCE

A GRICULTURE overshadows every other resource in this Island, and few countries, considering everything, are better adapted for profitable farming. No floods or tornadoes destroy the labors of its inhabitants, or mar its beauty.

"RENT BY NO RAVAGE BUT THE GENTLE PLOW"

The soil is light, warm and easily tilled, and its productiveness is, on the whole, equal to that of any other part of Canada. Very great progress has in recent times been made in this line. That agriculture will continue to be the great resource of this country, is certain.

The fisheries must always be one of the standard resources of Prince Edward Island. But the inclinations of the Islanders are so decidedly agricultural that the culture of the deep has not received from them the attention it deserves. The Island waters are of immense importance, and the mackerel fisheries in the " North Bay " are considered to be worth more than those on all the other eastern coasts of the Dominion combined.

One of the greatest sources of profit is the Lobster Fishery. This industry shows signs of deterioration from over-fishing ; but the strict enforcement of the regulations regarding the close season, which is from the 15th July until the 19th April inclusive, etc., is having a good effect.

The oyster fishery is extensive, is annually increasing and is capable of vast development. The employment by the Dominion Government, a few years ago, of an expert in this line has been, and will still be, productive of good results in the preservation and replenishing of the oyster beds. The close season is from the 1st June to the 15th September, inclusive.

Of two former resources not much can now be said. The forests, once extensive, have been reduced, although there, are still specimens of the principal trees, such as beech, birch pine, maple, poplar, spruce, fir, hemlock, larch and cedar. An approximate estimate of the area of forest and woodland in 1894 was : forest and woodland 797 square miles, woodland 39.85 per cent. Much of this, though wooded, is covered with small growth only.

Ship-building too, formerly a considerable resource, has declined here as it has done in other parts of the world.

THE FLORA AND FAUNA OF P. E. ISLAND
Flora

* " The sandstone swells of Prince Edward Island are everywhere clothed with a rich and varied vegetation. Its flora is much the same as spreads over the rest of Eastern Canada, but its dry and fertile soil produces a greater abundance of deciduous forest trees and the flowering plants which usually accompany them.

On the rolling districts, affording the best agricultural soils, Beech, Yellow Birch, Maple. Oak, and White Pine flourish, with an undergrowth of Mountain Maple, Rowan, Hazel, Elder. and thick-tangled brambles. Grasses carpet the soil, jeweled with roses, convolvuli, and sweet-scented violets. These plants belong to the Central Canadian Flora.

On the cold soils of the swamps and barrens a different class of vegetation abounds. Spruces and sparse-foliaged Larches, Poplars. Birches, Aspens, and moss-grown Firs form the timber growth ; while a thick, shrubby carpet of Andromeda, Ledum, Whortleberries, and prostrate Arbutus spreads at their feet. These are members of the Sub-Arctic Flora, inhabiting the far north of Canada and penetrating even within the Arctic Circle. Thus two distinct floras occupy the two distinct classes of soil common on the Island.

Other peculiarities are noticeable. The Cedar is confined to Prince County, and we never saw the Arum, the Calapogon, or the grand-flowered Habinaria in other parts of the Island. The Hemlock is not found east of St. Peter's. The assemblage of plants on the Triassic hills is something different from that on Permian districts. The sand dunes have a flora peculiar to themselves. And amid the surf-lashed skerries of our rocky coasts, the lover of nature will find a distinct field of study in the Algae, Fucoids, and Corrallins of marine growth."

Fauna

" The Fauna of Prince Edward Island is numerous and varied. A few larger animals, as the Moose, the Caribou, the Wolf, the Raccoon, and the Wolverine, which roam over the continental lands are excluded from the Island by its insular position. But this is much more than compensated by the numerous marine animals which inhabit our coasts, and which afford some of the most interesting studies of animal life."

Of swimming, wading, singing and other birds there are the genera common to most countries. Rabbits and squirrels are very numerous. The beaver, formerly met with is now unknown. Black bears and foxes, (particularly the silver-gray and black varieties) are rare, and the wild-cat or lynx once found, is now extinct. Wolves have been known to cross the Northumberland Straits on the ice to the Island.

---

* Bain's Natural History of P. E. Island, 1890

AGRICULTURE IN THE "GARDEN PROVINCE"
Its Importance

PRINCE EDWARD ISLAND has been aptly termed a "great million acre farm." It is essentially an agricultural province, not less than 80 per cent. of its total population being interested in this industry. It is the most thoroughly cultivated territory on this side of the Atlantic, and is one great garden from end to end. There were according to the census of 1891, 718,092 acres of improved lands of which 536,175 acres were under crop, 178,072 acres of pasture land, and 3,845 acres of gardens and orchards. The total amount of farm land assessed in 1898 was about 1,267,876 acres. The average size of the farms is 75 acres, and the average value $1,000. In 1891 the total number of farmers was 15,137, and including sons 20,227.

Agriculture is the main-stay of the Province and the importance of the industry cannot be over-estimated. A larger amount of capital is invested in this than in any other pursuit, namely: in lands, buildings, implements and stock about $22,000,000, as against $2,911,963 in trades and manufactures. In the production of milk, butter and cheese alone, there is invested in Prince Edward Island at least $1,325,600.

It is somewhat difficult to determine the annual value of the products of the farm in this Island, but the following figures at current market prices are probably nearly correct :—

Field products	$5,000,000
Live stock increase	500,000
Dairy produce	1,000,000
Orchard and Garden products	100,000
Pasture	400,000
Eggs, wool, honey, etc.	400,000
Total	$7,400,000

The following is taken from a pamphlet on Prince Edward Island issued by the Provincial Government in 1888:

"The Island is noted for the fertility of its soil, and it may confidently be asserted that, with the exception of a few bogs and swamps composed of a soft spongy turf, or a deep layer of wet black mould, the whole Island

"A GREAT MILLION ACRE FARM"

consists of highly valuable cultivable land. The soil, which is well watered with numerous springs and rivers, is formed for the most part of a rich layer of vegetable matter above a bright loam, resting upon a stiff clay and sandstone; the land in its natural state, being covered with timber and shrub of every variety. The under-lying rock through the main part of the Island, belongs to the upper Permian, capped about New London and Cavendish, with a triangular section of Triassic of considerable size; but in Prince County, west of Summerside, where the denudation has been greater, the lower Permian comes to the surface. All kinds of grain and vegetables grown in England ripen here in great perfection. The principal crops raised are wheat, oats, barley, potatoes, and turnips, of which oats and potatoes are exported in very large quantities. Mr. J. P. Sheldon, Professor of Agriculture at the Wilts and Hants Agricultural College, Downton, near Salisbury, who visited the Island in 1880, thus writes of it:—' In some respects this is one of the most beautiful Provinces in the Dominion, and it has probably the largest proportion of cultivable land. The soil generally is a red sandy loam, of one character throughout, but differing in quality. On the whole, the grass land of the Island and the character of the sward, consisting as it does of indigenous clovers and a variety of finer grasses, reminded me strongly of some portions of old England. The people, too, are more English in appearance than those of any other of the Provinces with the exception of New Brunswick. This is probably owing to a cooler climate, and the contiguity of the sea. Prince Edward Island is covered with a soil that is easy to cultivate, sound and healthy, capable of giving excellent crops of roots, grain and grass, an honest soil that will not fail to respond to the skill of the husbandman. The Island grows very good wheat, and probably better oats than most other parts of the Dominion. Of the former the crops are from 18 to 30 bushels, and of the latter 25 to 70 bushels per acre. Barley, too, makes a very nice crop. Wheat, at the time of my visit, was worth 4s. per bushel of 60 lbs., oats 1s. 9d. per bushel of 34 lbs., and barley 2s. 6d. to 3s. per bushel of 48 lbs. The Island is noted for its large crops of excellent potatoes, which not un-commonly foot up to 250 bushels an acre of fine handsome tubers. Swedes make a fine crop, not uncommonly reaching 750 bushels per acre of sound and solid bulbs.'

In addition to the natural fertility of the soil, the great facility for obtaining manure may be set down as one of the principal advantages. In most of the bays and rivers are found extensive deposits of musselmud, formed by decayed oyster, clam and mussel shells. These deposits vary from five to twenty feet in depth, and their surface is often several feet below low water level. Machines placed upon the ice and worked by horse power are used for raising this manure, which is then carried off by sleds and distributed over the fields while the covering of snow still remains. Procured in this way, in large quantities, and possessing great fertilizing qualities, it has vastly improved the agricultural status of the Island. An eminent authority, Sir J. W. Dawson, F. R. S. C. M. G., Principal and Vice-Chancellor of McGill University, Montreal, says :—' The great wealth of Prince Edward Island consists in its fertile soil, and the preservation of this in a productive state is an object of imperative importance. The ordinary soil of the Island is a bright, red loam, passing into stiff clay on the one hand, and sandy loam on the other. Naturally it contains all the mineral requisites for cultivated crops, while its abounding in peroxide of iron enables it rapidly to digest organic manures, and also to retain well their ammoniacal products. The chief natural manures afforded by the Island, and which may be used in addition to the farm manures to increase the fertility of the soil, or restore it when exhausted, are,—(1). *Mussel mud*, or oyster shell mud of the bays. Experience has proved this to be of the greatest value. (2). *Peat and marsh mud and swamp soil.* These afford organic matters to the run out soil, at a very cheap rate. (3). *Seaweed*, which can be obtained in large quantities on many parts of the shores, and is of great manural value, whether fresh or composted (4). *Fish offal.* The heads and bones of cod are more especially of much practical importance. (5). *Limestone.* The brown earthy limestones of the Island are of much value in affording a supply of this material, as well as small quantities of phosphates and alkalies. Where manures require to be purchased from abroad, those that will be found to produce the greatest effects are those capable of affording phosphates and alkalies, more especially bone earth, super-phosphates of lime and guano ; but when fish offal and seaweed can be procured in sufficient quantity, or when good dressings of the oyster deposit are applied, these foreign aids may well be dispensed with, at least for many years.' Of this deposit Professor Sheldon speaks as follows :—' The Island possesses one advantage which is unique and very valuable. I refer now to its thick beds of '' mussel mud '' or '' oyster mud,'' which are found in all bays and river mouths. The deposit, which is commonly many feet thick, consists of the organic remains of countless generations of oysters, mussels, clams, and other bivalves of the ocean, and of crustaceous animals generally. The shells are generally more or less intact, embedded in a dense deposit of mud-like stuff, which is found to be a fertilizer of singular value and potency. The supply of it is said to be almost inexhaustible, and it is indeed a mine of wealth to the Island. A good dressing of it secures fertility in a striking manner to the poorest soils ; clover grows after it quite luxuriously, and, as it were, indigenously by its aid heavy crops of turnips and potatoes are raised, and, indeed, it may be regarded as a manure of great value and applicable to any kind of crop. Nor is it soon exhausted, for the shells in it decay year by year, throwing off a film of fertilizing matter.' "

AGRICULTURAL PRODUCTS

According to the census of 1891, the proportion of oats and potatoes grown in the Province per thousand acres is higher than that of any part of Canada east of the Prairies, and the proportion of wheat, turnips and other crops and roots is equally high. The following figures indicate the progress made in farming during the last three-quarters of a century:—In 1825 there were raised 766 bushels of wheat, 10,717 bushels of oats, and 47,220 bushels of potatoes. In 1841 there were of wheat 160,028 bushels; of barley, 83,299; of oats, 611,824; of potatoes, 2,250,114 bushels; number of horses, 9,861; of neat cattle, 41,915; sheep, 73,650; hogs, 35,521.

In 1860 (as shown by the census of 1861) there were raised of wheat, 346.125 bushels; of barley, 223,195; oats, 2,218,578; buckwheat, 50,127; potatoes, 2,972,235; turnips, 348,784; hay, 31,000 tons; horses, 18,765; neat cattle, 60,015; sheep, 107,242; hogs, 71,535.

In the year 1890, the products included:—

Wheat, acres under cultivation 44,703, Yield, 596,761 bushels
Barley,   "   "   7,594,   "   147,880   "
Oats   "   "   123,924,   "   2,922,552   "
Buckwheat,   "   84,460   "
Potatoes, acres under cultivation 43,521,   "   7,071,308   "
Turnips,   "   "   4,411,   "   2,005,453   "
Hay,   "   "   150,108,   "   132,959 tons
Grass and Clover,   "   12,417 bushels
Corn,   "   2,651   "
Beans,   "   2,445   "
Peas,   "   4,735   "
Rye,   "   221   "

In 1881 there was grown in this Province 1,367 lbs. of Tobacco; in 1891, 795 lbs.; and in 1898, several tons.

The following table gives the yield per acre and present prices of certain products:—

	Weight per bushel	Bushels to the acre	Value
Wheat	60 lbs.	16 to 20	$ 0.70 to 0.90
Oats	34 lbs.	30 to 40	0.35 to 0.40
Barley	48 lbs.	25 to 35	0.45 to 0.55
Potatoes	60 lbs	150 to 250	0.18 to 0.30
Turnips	60 lbs.	400 to 1,000	0.12 to 0.16

AS A STOCK-RAISING COUNTRY

STEADY improvement is being made in the raising of farm stock. Excellent specimens are to be met with in every section, and they enjoy immunity from disease to a very large degree.

	Census of 1891	Estimates 1898
Horses	25,674	30,000
Colts and Fillies	11,718	14,060
Milch Cows	45,849	55,017
Working Oxen	116	138
Other horned Cattle	45,730	54,876
Sheep	147,372	176,800
Swine	42,629	51,100
Hens	485,580	582,700

Cattle

Owing to the ease with which turnips, potatoes, oats, &c., are raised, coupled with the excellence of the hay crop, Prince Edward Island is exceedingly well adapted for cattle feeding. The following breeds are well established : Shorthorn, Ayrshire, Jersey, Guernsey, Holstein, Aberdeen and Angus. The increased quantity and superior quality of the fodder resulting from the application of mussel mud to the land has produced great improvement in the quality of cattle.

Horses

Prince Edward Island is noted for a fine class of horses, much attention having been bestowed upon their breeding. The leading pure breeds are as follows: Clydesdale, Shire, Percheron, Trotting Standard Bred.

Owing to early Government importations of thoroughbred and cart Stallions, which have more recently been followed by many private purchases from abroad, the horses are regarded as among the best in America, and command ready sale at good prices. In exhibitions of late years held in different parts of the Dominion, Island horses have received a large share of the honors and prizes awarded.

Sheep

This country is well adapted for sheep, the soil being light, dry and sound, growing a thick-set, tender and nutritious herbage. The mutton is of excellent flavor, and the export of sheep and lambs to the other provinces and to the United States is assuming large proportions. The leading breeds are : Leicester, Cotswold, Shropshire, Oxford Down, Southdown.

Swine

Great advances are being made in the raising of swine, and the principal breeds are : Yorkshire, Berkshire, Tamworth, Poland China, Duroc Jersey.

Near Charlottetown are two up-to-date farms. One is the Heartz farm of over 300 acres, which produced last year in addition to pasturing its cattle and horses, 300 tons of corn and ensilage, 20,000 bushels of turnips and mangels; 600 bushels of wheat which was sold for seed ; and enough hay, oats, etc., to feed the stock. On the farm are 100 head of milch cows, 60 head of young cattle, all pure bred Jerseys, Guernseys, and Holsteins, and 40 horses. The Creamery in connection with the farm produced last year 100,000 lbs. of Butter. The other is the Eastview Farm of over 200 acres of good pasture land, and on it are bred pure Guernsey Cattle. Besides these, there are many model farms throughout the Province.

A stock farm devoted to the breeding of horses, cattle, sheep and swine, is maintained by the Provincial Government, and the yearly surplus stock is divided among the three counties.

FRUIT GROWING

THE old idea that fruit could not be grown in this country has been exploded. This industry is now receiving more attention than formerly. There is considerable raised, and the country generally appears to be well adapted to its cultivation. The most abundant kinds are apples, plums, and cherries. Small fruits such as strawberries, raspberries, and gooseberries, etc., are also grown, and the culture of cranberries on the waste bog lands is increasing. Cultivated strawberries, wild raspberries and blueberries are exported to some extent. Prior to 1898 there was very little export of fruit, but in the fall of that year, owing to the subsidizing of ocean steamers, fitted with cold storage for direct service between this Province and Great Britain, several successful shipments of apples were made to the old country, and there can be no doubt about the possibilities of the extension of the industry. The shipments have commanded good prices. With more careful selection and better packing of the fruit, together with good transportation and storage facilities, this trade can be vastly extended and made very remunerative.

The interests of the Fruit-growers are carefully fostered by the Prince Edward Island Fruit Growers' Association, an Institution incorporated in 1898. Its objects, like those of all similar societies elsewhere, are co-operative and educational. It disseminates information as to the best methods of culture and as to proper handling, packing, and marketing, and also promotes legislation in the interests of the industry Connected with the Association are some of the most prominent and scientific Fruit-growers of the Province.

There were raised in 1891, of apples 52,018 bushels; plums 1,479 bushels; and cherries 4,265 bushels.

The yield in 1898 was estimated to be :—

Apples	65,030	bushels
Plums	1,850	"
Cherries	5,330	"
Pears	90	"
Other fruits	3,090	"

THE DAIRY INDUSTRY

ONE of the most important branches of agriculture is the dairy industry. Since 1891 there has been great improvement in this line. An experimental station for the manufacture of cheese started in 1892 under the supervision of the Dominion Dairy Commissioner, was followed in the succeeding years by several other factories, all, with one exception, being on the co-operative principle, each company owning its building and plant. Since then 34 cheese factories (of which 16 are also creameries and 4 are separating stations) and 7 creameries have been established throughout the Province.

The exception just mentioned is that of a Charlottetown gentleman who imported a large number of pure-bred Holstein, Guernsey, and Jersey cattle, and started the manufacture of butter in a factory of his own. There are also three other creameries now owned and operated as private enterprises. This new industry is well adapted to the Province. The products are admitted to be first-class and have found a ready sale in the markets of Great Britain, Newfoundland, and the West Indies.

These factories originally managed by the Dominion Government are, with the exception of the four creameries above mentioned, now conducted by Joint Stock Companies of farmers. Prince Edward Island derived last year from the Dairy Industry the sum of $364,557.63.

The factories are located as follows :—

Cheese Factories

Abram's Village   Alberton

Campbellton
† Cornwall
* Dunk River
East River
Emerald
Gowan Brae
Grand River
* Hampton
* Hazel Brook
* Hillsboro
* Kensington
Lakeville
* Marshfield
* Montague
Morell
* Mount Stewart

* Murray Harbor North
* Murray Harbor South
* New Dominion
† New Glasgow
* New Perth
O'Leary
* Orwell
* Red House
St. Eleanor's
* St. George's
St. Peter's
† Stanley
Tignish
* Vernon River Bridge
† Wiltshire
Winsloe

Creameries

Central, Charlottetown
Charlottetown
Central, Summerside (with separating station at Freetown
Crapaud, (with separating station at Bonshaw)
Lot 16
Park Corner
Tryon

In all 41 Incorporated Dairying Associations.

CHEESE

The development of the Cheese Industry has been remarkable. In the summer of 1896, the cheese manufactured and sold in the Province amounted to 1,612,209 lbs. valued at $141,235,19. 34 factories made cheese in 1898, 16 made butter also, and there were 7 Creameries. In 1898 there were 2,816,045 lbs. of cheese manufactured valued at $229,249.17.

BUTTER

The Butter Industry is not so advanced as that of the

---

* Also a creamery.
† Also a separating station.

cheese, owing to the lack of proper facilities for getting the product on the market in prime condition. Prince Edward Island is capable of producing a very fine quality of butter and with the proper means of manufacture, packing and transportation, there is every prospect of this product competing successfully in the British market with the article from other countries. In the summer of 1896 and winter of 1897 the output of the butter factories amounted to 225,802 lbs. the value of which was $41,706.37. In 1898, the quantity of butter made in 25 factories was 746,544 lbs. or over 373 tons, valued at $135,308.46   Many factories are now making butter during the winter season, and cheese during the summer, and the number of creameries is steadily increasing.

The average yield of butter from milk passed through the separator is about 4 lbs. for every 10 gallons of milk of 10 lbs. each; so that the average cow produces annually from 150 to 200 lbs. of butter or 400 to 450 lbs. of cheese. The yield of milk from fairly good milking cattle is approximately 400 to 500 galls. per annum, although from 600 to 800 galls. per head are frequently obtained from selected herds. The rate paid for milk at the factories at present prices of cheese should average between 75 and 80 cts. per 100 lbs.

INDIAN CORN

The growth of Indian corn for fodder has been greatly extended on this Island. In 1890, the area devoted to this article was not more than 10 acres. In 1896, it was estimated that the area of Indian corn for fodder was about 10,000 acres. Many farmers have built silos, and others stook the corn for feeding during the winter season.

EXHIBITIONS

Exhibitions of live stock, farm, garden and dairy produce, and manufactures have for a number of years, been held at Charlottetown, Summerside, Georgetown and other places. The Provincial Fair at Charlottetown in connection with horse races under the auspices of the Driving Park Association, which up to 1897 was held annually, is from an agricultural point of view, superior to any show of the kind in the Maritime Provinces.

PRINCE EDWARD ISLAND FARM METHODS

In agricultural matters old methods are rapidly giving place to new. Following the example of other countries, many P. E. Island farmers are now bestowing attention upon the higher branches of agriculture, or in other words turning their raw material into a finished product, instead of marketing it as such. They are now feeding their coarse grain to live stock instead of selling it, and are producing butter, cheese, meat, poultry and fruits for the British market. This change will preserve the fertility of the soil, and give better returns for the labor and skill expended. Still, the average P. E. Island husbandman remains a general or mixed farmer, and specialists are relatively few.

FARMING WEATHER

The summer season is very favorable for farming operations in Prince Edward Island. Although the tedious springs retard to a certain extent the early work, yet seeding is generally through by the first of June. The summer is short and the crops rapidly grow to maturity—first hay, then barley closely followed by wheat and oats. After the close of October, outside work is practically at an end, and from then until the beginning of April the farmer has comparatively little to do except attend to his stock, and haul wood, mussel-mud, etc.

The farmers of this Province are worthy of their fair heritage. They are an industrious, independent and moral people, and are generally a well-to-do class. The typical husbandman is a plain hardworking and law-abiding citizen. As a rule, the farms and houses are characterized by great neatness.

LEGISLATION AFFECTING AGRICULTURE

At the session of the Legislative Assembly in 1898, an Act was passed for the establishment of a Department of Agriculture. This Department it is expected will shortly be inaugurated.

The Domestic Animals' Act, passed in 1888, with a later amendment, restricts the running at large of certain animals and provides for the arrest and sale of animals unlawfully at

A TYPICAL P. E. ISLAND FARM

large. An Act passed in 1881 contains provisions to prevent injury by dogs.

In regard to Dairying, provision is made by the Farmers' and Dairymen's Association Act of 1892 for the organizing of two Branch Societies in each Electoral District of the Province. The Provincial Government appropriates a small sum per annum for the use of each society. These Societies have for their object the advancement of dairying and agriculture generally throughout the Province.

An Act passed in 1895 provides for the incorporation of Cheese and Butter Manufacturing Associations, under which statute many companies have been organized.

A measure for the prevention of the spread of black-knot on plum and cherry trees was enacted in 1895.

An Act for the incorporation of the "The Agricultural Cold Storage Company" was passed in 1896, and another to encourage the construction of a cold storage warehouse was placed on the statute book in 1897.

The following legislation was passed at the session of 1899 :

An Act incorporating the Prince Edward Island Dairying Association, providing for the encouragement of Dairying and improvement in the manufacture of butter and cheese and all matters connected therewith. Also for the appointment of a Dairy Instructor and Inspector part of whose salary is paid by the Provincial Government, and also authorizing the establishment of a Dairymen's Board of Trade.

An Act respecting Tuberculosis in Cattle which authorizes the appointment of an Inspector whose duty it shall be to examine all cattle brought into the Province for breeding grazing, feeding or dairying purposes, and to detain such in quarantine unless accompanied by a certificate or affidavit of freedom from disease.

A further amendment to the Act for the Reclamation of Marsh Lands.

The Provincial Government pays half of the remuneration of a horticultural expert who is spraying, grafting and pruning fruit trees on the Island this season.

DRAINAGE, DYKING, ETC.

Acts were passed in 1881, 1895, and 1898 for the appointment of Commissioners of Sewers and the reclamation of the large tracts of marsh land that exist throughout the Province, for the purpose of rendering the same available for cultivation.

As a result of such legislation, Aboideaux (which have been more or less successful) have been constructed at the undermentioned places :—

	Length	Acreage drained
Mount Stewart	100 feet	500
Fullerton's Marsh	300 "	120
Dunk River	100 "	220
Pisquid River (not completed)		

ITS FISHERIES

PRINCE EDWARD ISLAND is the best fishing station in the Gulf of Saint Lawrence, and the fisheries, particularly those on the north coast, are exceedingly valuable. They consist principally of mackerel, lobsters, herring, cod, hake, and oysters. Salmon, bass, shad, halibut and trout are caught in limited quantities.

The yield and value of the Fisheries of this Province for 1897 was as follows :—

Kinds of Fish		Quantity	Price	Value
			$ cts.	$ cts.
Salmon,	lbs.	5,000	0.20	1,000.00
Herring, salted,	brls.	28,364	4.00	113,456.00
" fresh,	lbs.	267,974	0.01	2,679.74
" smoked,	lbs.	400	0.02	8.00
Mackerel, salted,	brls.	1,976	15.00	29,640.00
" fresh,	lbs.	16,088	0.12	1,930.56
Lobsters, preserved in cans,	lbs.	2,466,682	0.20	493,336.40
Cod, dried,	cwt.	20,352	4.00	81,408.00
Cod, tongues and sounds,	brls.	67½	10.00	675.00
Haddock, fresh,	lbs.	5,100	0.03	153.00
" dried,	cwt.	715	3.00	2,145.00
Hake, dried,	cwt.	10,088	2.25	22,698.00
" sounds,	lbs.	20,883	0.50	10,416.50
Halibut,	lbs.	5,100	0.10	510.00
Trout,	lbs.	31,750	0.10	3,175.00
Smelts,	lbs.	598,543	0.05	29,927.15
Alwives, salted	brls.	810	4.00	3,240.00
Eels,	brls.	1,547	10.00	15,470.00
Oysters,	brls.	20,915	4.00	83,660.00
Tom cod,	lbs.	31,850	0.05	1,592.50
Squid,	brls.	980	4.00	3,920.00
Coarse and mixed fish,	brls.	160	2.00	320.00
Fish Oil,	galls.	12,117	0.30	3,635.10
Fish as bait,	brls.	31,589	1.50	47,383.50
Fish as manure,	brls.	3,370	0.50	1,685.00
Fish guano,	tons.	885	1.00	885.00
			Total	$ 954,949 45

The number of vessels and boats engaged in the Fisheries in 1897 was 2,059, and the number of men about 4,720. The number of lobster canneries was 220, number of traps 216,133, number of smoke and fish houses 45, number of piers and wharfs 29, and the number of men employed 2,631. The value of the lobster plant was $243.022, and of the other fishery fixtures $23,440. The value of the boats, vessels, and other apparatus was $119,694.

The yield of Lobsters, Oysters and Mackerel for 1898 was as follows:—Lobsters, 42,112 cases; Oysters, 29,800 bbls.; Mackerel, 3,149 bbls.

The Malpeque Oysters are famous, bearing the same relation to Prince Edward Island and Canada generally, as the " Blue Points" and "Cherry Stones" do to Americans.

Quahaugs are being fished and shipped principally from Prince County, and this industry bids fair to assume considerable proportions.

In order to encourage sea-fishing and the building of fishing vessels, the Dominion Government by Acts passed in 1882 and 1891, provides for the distribution of $160.000 annually among the fishermen and vessels of Canada. This bounty is paid under certain restrictions, on the basis of $3 a ton to vessels, $3 per man to boat fishermen, and $1 per boat to the owners. The total bounty paid in Prince Edward Island in 1897 was $9,809; the number of claims paid was 1,171; the number of vessels receiving bounty was 20; the number of men, 109; and amount paid $1,144; number of boats receiving bounty 1,151; number of men, 2,147, and amount paid $8,665.

COMMERCE AND SHIPPING

Commerce is maintained principally with the other Maritime Provinces, the United States and Great Britain. The volume of Exports is large. They embrace oats, potatoes, butter, cheese, eggs, live stock, oysters, lobsters, mackerel and other products of the field and fisheries. Trade with the mother-land is growing and the large inter-provincial traffic is increasing. Considerable pork, beef and mutton is shipped during the winter to Nova Scotia and New Brunswick; and large quantities of smelts, etc., go to Boston and other American cities.

FOREIGN EXPORTS

The total value of Foreign Exports for the year ending 31st December, 1898, (in addition to Canadian export and home consumption) was as follows:—

Total Fisheries - -	$ 506,501
Forest - - - -	597
Animals and their produce	474,644
Agricultural products, etc. -	343,305
Total	$ 1,325,047

An estimate of the shipments of Eggs, for 1898 is 1,550,000, dozen, valued at $147,250, which amount is included in the foregoing. Much produce and live stock is carried by steamer and small craft to different Provincial ports, statistics regarding which it is difficult to obtain.

IMPORTS

The imports for the year ending 31st December, 1898, as nearly as can be determined, amounted in value to $477,269. Owing to the manner in which the Customs Returns, as published, are made up, it is impossible to ascertain the actual imports of the Island. Large quantities of goods are purchased duty paid in Montreal, Toronto, Halifax, St. John and other Canadian points and consumed in Prince Edward Island, for which this Province does not receive credit.

PRINCE EDWARD ISLAND'S MARKETS

The question of increasing the trade relations of Prince Edward Island with the outside world, more particularly the marketing of its agricultural products, is a very important one. The present Federal Government is inaugurating a complete system of Cold Storage, which will enable Canadian produce to be delivered in England in good condition. In the benefits of this, Prince Edward Island has already participated, ocean steamships fitted with cold storage having made three trips between the Island and Great Britain in the fall of 1898.

These shipments were very successful, and it is expected that the great boon of direct steamship service between this Province and the Old Country will be afforded permanently.

The shipments by these steamers were as follows :—

S. S. "Lake Winnipeg" for Liverpool, 23rd September :

4431 boxes Cheese	21 barrels Apples
414 boxes Butter	18 boxes Losters
777 cases Eggs	5 barrels Oysters
478 bales Hay	690 Sheep and Lambs
177 sacks Oats	5 head Cattle

4 Horses

Total value of Cargo $35,148

S. S. "Lake Winnipeg" for Liverpool, 12th November :

2337 boxes Cheese	1482 cases Canned Meats
1044 packages Butter	51 boxes Hog Products
1204 cases Eggs	40 barrels Vegetables
1009 bales Hay	18 boxes Potatoes
249 barrels Apples	1228 Sheep
169 boxes Lobsters	91 head Cattle
54 barrels Oysters	8 horses

Total Value of Cargo $60,000

S. S. "Gaspesia" for Liverpool, 25th December :

1265 cases Canned Meats	24 boxes Lobsters
626 boxes and tubs Butter	238 barrels Apples
6 tons Poultry	300 tons Hay
100 tons Bacon	10,000 bushels Oats
96 carcases Mutton	138 bags bones
25 dressed Hogs	1 barrel Oysters
6 quarters Beef	1 bag Seed
10 barrels Pork	1286 Sheep
105 boxes Cheese	85 head Cattle

Total Value of Cargo $50,756.70

TONNAGE STATISTICS

The following table shows the Tonnage of Vessels, British and Foreign, employed in the coasting trade which arrived at and departed from Prince Edward Island from 1876 to 1898 :

Year	Tons	Year	Tons
1876	883,502	1888	1,120,815
1877	929,864	1889	1,194,020
1878	862,418	1890	1,243,993
1879	559,984	1891	1,139,178
1880	628,742	1892	1,271,638
1881	951,632	1893	1,198,539
1882	902,269	1894	1,120,383
1883	1,006,481	1895	1,118,491
1884	910,175	1896	1,310,339
1885	1,157,575	1897	1,209,602
1886	891,633	1898	1,182,180
1887	1,151,023		

Statement of Registered Sea-going tonnage carrying cargo into and out of the Province by five year periods, with yearly averages and percentages of increase or decrease :—

Period	Total Tonnage	Yearly Average	Per cent.
1874-78	666,351	133,270	
1879-83	628,596	125,719	− 5.7
1884-88	636,135	127,227	+ 1.2
1889-93	499,581	99,916	− 21.4
1894		104,710	+ 4.8
1895		123,791	+18.2
1896		116,469	− 5.9
1897		107,960	− 7.3
1898		142,899	+32.3

Registered Sea-going Tonnage carrying cargo into the Province :—

Period	Total Tonnage	Yearly Average	Per cent.
1874-78	296,301	59,260	
1879-83	248,167	49,633	− 16.2
1884-88	253,983	50,797	+ 2.3
1889-93	198,327	39,665	− 21.9
1894		40,692	+ 2.6
1895		46,218	+13.6
1896		43,255	− 6.4
1897		39,278	− 9.0
1898		54,051	+37.6

Registered sea-going tonnage carrying cargo out of the
Province :—

Period	Total Tonnage	Yearly Average	Per cent.
1874-78	370,050	74,010	
1879-83	380,429	76,086	+ 2.8
1884-88	382,152	76 430	+ 0.4
1889-93	301,254	60,251	− 21.1
1894		64,018	+ 6.3
1895		77,573	+21.5
1896		73,214	− 5.3
1897		68,682	− 6.2
1893		88,848	+29.4

ITS CITY AND TOWNS

CHARLOTTETOWN, the Capital, and the third in size
of the cities "of the Maritime," was founded by Morris
and Deschamp in 1768, and was incorporated in 1855.
It is situated at the confluence of the York, Elliot and
Hillsborough Rivers, and possesses one of the finest harbors
in the world. It is the principal shipping-port of the "Garden
Province," and has a thriving trade. This city is the eastern
terminus of the Plant Steamship Line, and it is a port of call for
the boats of the Quebec Steamship Company, plying between
Montreal and Gulf of St. Lawrence Ports. The "City of
Ghent" makes weekly round trips between here and Halifax,
and there are several local lines. One of the healthiest towns
in Canada, it is yearly becoming more desirable as a place of
residence. A system of Water Works constructed in 1887-88,
at a cost of $165,000, furnishes water that is unsurpassed in
excellence in America, pumped direct from a spring, and there
is a modern system of sewerage. The city is generously laid
out, its streets being wide and many of them shaded, and its
four public squares are well kept.

Queen Square in the centre of the town is one of the
prettiest open spaces in the Dominion. In summer it is a
very attractive spot with its beautifully arranged flower beds,

CHARLOTTETOWN FROM FORT EDWARD

sparkling fountain and band stand. Many improvements have been made in Charlottetown in recent years, and it is gradually assuming the appearance of a modern city. The wooden buildings that served as business establishments a generation ago have given place to brick and stone structures, and similar progress is to be seen in the residential districts. The city's surroundings are beautiful, and the suburbs are charming with gardens, groves and hedges of evergreen, with shaded roads and fertile fields. Pleasant drives through pretty pastoral scenery, and enjoyable excursions on rivers and bay are among the attractions of Charlottetown. Horses for driving, sail and row boats can be hired at very cheap rates.

One of the most beautiful spots and probably the place of greatest historic interest on the Island is Warren Farm at Rocky Point, nearly opposite the city and within a few minutes trip by ferry. This was originally Port La Joie, the former Capital and the residence of several distinguished people under the French Regime. First settled by the French in 1720, it was allowed to decay, but in 1749 the place was resuscitated and new buildings erected. Grass-covered mounds and excavations are all that now remain of the forts, the village of several hundred inhabitants, church, ecclesiastical establishment, governor's residence, etc., that once existed. The principal fort designed and laid off by the French and afterwards constructed by the English, was called Fort Amherst. Many relics have been found, and the old cellars, outlines of the earthworks and burial ground, can be distinctly seen. The air of romance that clings to the spot, the fine view from the site of Fort Amherst, with the still more beautiful outlook from "Ringwood" on the elevation west of the fort, and the presence of an Indian encampment near by, make the locality decidedly interesting.

The principal buildings are on or in the vicinity of Queen Square. The Post Office and Custom House is a massive brick and stone structure, and in it are also the Savings Bank and other Federal Government Offices. The Provincial Building contains the Local Government Offices, and Legislative Assembly Chamber, etc. This edifice is of Nova Scotia freestone, and the corner stone was laid on May 16th, 1843.

QUEEN SQUARE

Adjoining the Provincial Building is the Law Courts.

Charlottetown is well supplied with places of worship, among which are one Roman Catholic, two Anglican, two Methodist, two Presbyterian, and two Baptist Churches. The Roman Catholic Diocese is located here, and authority over the spiritual affairs of the Church of England is exercised by the Bishop of Nova Scotia. The new Saint Dunstan's Cathedral is one of the finest Churches in the Lower Provinces, and Saint Paul's Church (Anglican) and Saint James' (Presbyterian) are beautiful buildings. The Chapel of Saint Peter's Cathedral is worthy of a visit. Other prominent structures are the Prince of Wales College, Bishop's Palace, City Hall, Masonic Temple, the Prince Edward Island and Charlottetown Hospitals, and the Public Schools.

The Charlottetown market is the admiration of strangers. Twice a week are here offered for sale the beautiful rich cream, butter, vegetables and other farm and market garden products for which the Island is so famous. The following are minimum are maximum market prices:

Apples 3c to 12c per dozen, and from 20c to 75c per bushel; Barley 35c to 65c per bushel; Brant 50c to 70c a pair; Beef, live weight, 3c to 5c per lb.; Beef, small, 5c to 12c per lb.; Butter fresh, from 15c in summer to 25c in winter; Butter, tub, 15c to 20c per lb.; Beans, green, 4c per lb.; Blueberries 3c to 7c per quart; Black Currants 8c to 15c per quart; Beets 25c to 40c per bushel; Cabbages 12c to 30c a dozen; Celery 3c to 7c per head; Cheese 12c to 20c per lb.; Codfish, fresh, 5c to 15c each according to size; Codfish, corned, 3c to 12c each; Corn, green, 12c for a dozen ears; Cranberries 8c to 14c per quart; Carrots 25c to 50c per bushel; Ducks 40c to 60c a pair; Fresh Eggs 7c to 25c a dozen according to the season; Fowls 30c to 60c a pair; Flour, Island made, $1.75 to $2.00 per cwt.; Gooseberries 8c to 15c per quart; Hides 5c to 7c per lb.; Hay 35c to 70c per cwt.; Hake 4c to 12c each; Herring 5c to 10c per dozen; Huckleberries 8c to 12c per quart; Lamb 30c to 60c per quarter carcass; Lobsters 5c to 10c each; Mackerel, fresh, 8c to 15c each according to supply; Oats 25c to 30c per bushel; Oatmeal $1.75 to $2.00 per cwt.; Onions 2c to 5c per lb.; Green Peas 10c to 15c per quart; Potatoes 16c to 30c per bushel; Pork 3c to 6c per lb.; Young Pigs $1.00 to $3.00 each; Parsnips 20c to 30c per bushel; Partridges 25c to 40c a pair; Radishes 3c a bunch; Raspberries 5c to 10c per quart; Red Currants 10c to 20c per quart; Sheep pelts 40c to 60c each; Straw $1.25 to $3.00 per load; Strawberries 10c to 20c per quart; Smelts 3c to 5c per dozen; Sausages 12c per lb.; Turkeys 60c to $1.50; Turnips 16c to 20c per bushel;

"ST. DUNSTAN'S CATHEDRAL"

Tomatoes. green, 10c per peck ; Veal 8c per lb. ; Wild Geese 50c to 80c each. The cheapness of provisions, &c., and the moderate house rents, ranging in Charlottetown from $80 to $200, combine to render this city a desirable place of residence for those of comparatively limited means.

The Institutions of Charlottetown include two well-conducted Hospitals (a Protestant and a Roman Catholic), an Insane Asylum, the Prince of Wales College and Normal School, which will shortly be housed in a handsome brick and stone building now in course of erection, Saint Dunstan's Roman Catholic College, two Convent schools, three large public schools, a Kindergarten and school of music, and several excellent private schools. A quarantine station or hospital for infectious diseases is under the control of the Dominion authorities. There is a well-appointed Young Men's Christian Association. A modern Opera House furnishes amusement for the theatre-going population.

Victoria Park, connected with the City by the Park Boulevard, contains 46 acres and possesses many beauty spots. Nearer the City is Government House. The Exhibition Grounds and Driving Park, and the Charlottetown Athletic Association Property contain good racing tracks, that of the former being pronounced one of the best in the Lower Provinces. Our illustration shows a race day in the Driving Park.

CHARLOTTETOWN DRIVING PARK

The city has two electric light plants, an electric fire alarm and a gas light and power company; and legislation has recently been passed for an electric street railway. There are three daily and several weekly and bi-weekly newspapers; and an interesting little monthly magazine has lately appeared upon the scene. Religious and National Societies are well represented, there being no less than 15 lodges or societies including Masons and Odd Fellows. The leading hotels are the Davies, Queen and Revere.

Charlottetown contains machine shops, wood-working, furniture and tobacco factories, a pork factory, woolen and flour mills, a boot and shoe factory, a condensed milk factory, and minor industries.

The number of establishments in 1881 and 1891, was:—

	1881	1891
Number	198	238
Capital	$980,018	$959,589
Number of hands employed	1,005	1,049
Wages paid	$235,241	$281,119
Cost of material	$610,209	$797,795
Value of products	$998,530	$1,405,246
Value per head of population	$ 87	$ 123

The city's affairs are managed by a Mayor and eight Councillors, and its population is about 12,000.

Summerside, in Prince County, has a population of about 3,000 and ranks next to the capital in wealth and importance. It is situated on Bedeque Bay, in the centre of one of the finest farming districts in the Province, and has a large trade being the principal oyster mart of the Island. It possesses a good harbor, and during the season of navigation has daily communication by steamer with New Brunswick. The town is lighted by electricity and boasts of the largest and finest departmental store in the Maritime Provinces. Its schools are excellent and hotels fair. Near Summerside is the Dunk River, a noted trout-fishing stream, where many piscatorial beauties have been killed. Alberton at the western end of the Province possesses the only harbor, Cascumpec Bay, available on a long line of coast, which has been considerably improved by dredging. The village has a good trade and a number of enterprising merchants. Thirty miles east of Charlottetown is Georgetown the winter port of the Island. It is situated at the junction of the Cardigan and Brudenell Rivers, has a magnificent harbor, and is one of the pleasantest places at which to take a summer outing in the Province. Souris the eastern terminus of the Railway, is sixty miles from Charlottetown. It has a good harbor and a large trade. One of the most beautiful villages on the Island, it is yearly becoming more popular as a summer resort. The other important places are, Tignish, Kensington, Montague, Mount Stewart and Victoria, all having the advantage of water connections or Railway Stations.

"WHERE MANY PISCATORIAL BEAUTIES HAVE BEEN KILLED"

LAND AND WATER ROUTES, &c.

HE Prince Edward Island Railway is a narrow gauge road 210 miles long, traversing the country from end to end, and touching almost every point of any importance. Its general offices are at Charlottetown. A branch to the Murray Harbor District in the southern part of the Province, with a bridge across the Hillsborough River, is to be constructed. Good waggon roads are everywhere found. During the season of navigation, there is daily communication by the fine steamers "Northumberland" and "Princess" of the Charlottetown Steam Navigation Company, between Summerside and Point du Chene, N. B. and Charlottetown and Pictou, N. S. This company was first organized in 1863, and it is worthy of remark that during these 36 years not an accident has occured by which a passenger or a piece of freight has been injured.

After the close of navigation, open communication is maintained between Georgetown and Pictou by the Steamer "Stanley," a boat specially designed for the winter work, and which has been wonderfully successful. The "Stanley" was built at Govan, on the Clyde, in 1888. She is constructed throughout of Siemen's-Martin steel. Her dimensions are :—Length 207 feet, breadth 32 feet, depth 20 feet 3 inches. She is a screw boat of 914 tons gross, and 300 horse power, and attains a speed of nearly 15 knots in clear water. Within the present year it is expected that the "Minto" a larger and more powerful boat than the "Stanley," will be ready to act in conjunction with her. In mid-winter the work of the steamers is supplemented by the Ice Boat Service between Cape Traverse on the Island and Cape Tormentine on the New Brunswick shore, a distance of about nine miles.

The standard ice-boat is 18 feet long, 5 feet wide and 2 feet 2 inches deep. Its frame is oaken, it is planked with cedar, and the planks are covered with tin. It has a double keel which serves for runners, and four leather straps are attached to each side. The crews are hardy, powerful and courageous men. The passage usually occupies three and a half hours, but when there is much "lolly" (small particles of ice floating in the water often to the depth of several feet), and

TWIN-SCREW STEAMER "NORTHUMBERLAND"

when wind and tide are unfavorable, it sometimes requires from five to seven hours. A trip by "the Capes" is a unique experience.

Freight and passenger steamers connect weekly with Quebec, Montreal, St. John's, Newfoundland, Halifax, Boston and the Magdalen Islands. Small steamers and sailing packets, most of them more or less subsidized, furnish means of coast and river transit. A direct steamship service to Great Britain was inaugurated in the fall of 1898.

Telegraphic communication is maintained by the cable of the Anglo-American Telegraph Company, 12 miles long, between Capes Traverse and Tormentine, and 27 other offices of this company are established throughout the Province and along the Railway. The land line is 130 miles long. This system also includes 1 mile of cable under the Hillsborough River at Charlottetown.

A telephone system of about 500 miles, reaching almost every important point is also in existence. Mails are despatched daily to the mainland and weekly to Great Britain, while advantage is taken of intervening opportunities to Europe viâ New York. There are good postal facilities throughout the Province, offices being established at intervals of three or four miles.

The following table gives the distances between Charlottetown and some of the principal cities of Canada and the United States, and the time required to make the journey during the summer season :—

		Miles	Hours	
Charlottetown to	Halifax, N. S.	160	12	
"	Moncton, N. B.	110	6	20 min.
"	St. John, N. B.	200	9	20 min.
"	Quebec, (I. C. R.)	600	23	
"	Montreal, (I. C. R.)	772	28	
"	Montreal, (C. P. R.)	681	25	
"	Ottawa, (C. A.)	887	31	
"	Ottawa, (C. P. R)	796	28	
"	Toronto, (G. T. R.)	1,105	37	
"	Toronto, (C. P. R.)	1,019	35	
"	Boston,	654	24	

STEAMER "PRINCESS"

		Miles	Hours
Charlottetown to	New York,	880	30
"	Philadelphia,	970	32
"	Vancouver,	3,584	124

THE ISLAND'S FINANCIAL INSTITUTIONS

THE Island Province possesses few financial institutions. Its banks are the Merchants of Prince Edward Island and the Summerside Bank. The former occupies a substantial building in Charlottetown, and does a very successful business. It was incorporated in 1871 and has Agencies at Souris Montague and Alberton. The Summerside Bank has been in existence for upwards of 30 years. Both are sound financial concerns. The Union Bank of Prince Edward Island, incorporated in 1863, was amalgamated with the Bank of Nova Scotia in 1883, and is now known as the Charlottetown Agency of that great Nova Scotian Institution. There is also a branch at Summerside. Another Halifax Bank, the Merchants, has agencies at Charlottetown and Summerside. A branch of the Dominion Government Savings Bank is established at Charlottetown, in which the amount to the credit of depositors at 1st July, 1899, was $1,800,666.92. There are Post Office Savings Banks at Summerside, Souris, Montague, Crapaud and Tignish. An Agency of the "Credit Foncier Franco Canadien' of Quebec does business at Charlottetown. There are no Loan or Trust Companies.

MERCHANTS AND MANUFACTURES

The business men of Prince Edward Island are up-to-date. Stores with well-selected stocks are found in every village and at many of the "cross-roads" throughout the country. In Charlottetown the establishments of all kinds are equal to those of any city of its size in Canada, and the window dressing of many of the stores is excellent. The principal dry goods retailers send buyers direct to England for their stocks, while the large army of commercial ambassadors who regularly visit the Island, secure substantial orders. In the Capital are several shipping firms, eight or nine dry goods establishments (some with wholesale departments) seven drug stores, two furniture factories and warerooms, five tailoring establishments, and several stores each in the lines of groceries, hardware, boots and shoes, etc. Summerside, too, possesses excellent business establishments. The Charlottetown Board of Trade is an influential body and is accomplishing good work for the city and province.

Manufactures are limited but are steadily developing. They include butter, cheese, starch, and soap factories, tanneries, grist, saw, and woolen mills, furniture factories, lobster and other canning establishments, carriage factories, etc.

By the census of 1891, the figures of Island industries were as follows:—

Number of Industrial Establishments,	2,679
Capital invested	$2,911,963
Number of hands employed,	7,910
Yearly wages about,	$1.101,620
Value of products,	$4,345,910

An increase compared with the census of 1881 of over 25 per cent. in the number of establishments, nearly 40 per cent. in capital invested, 38 per cent. in the number of hands employed, and 27 per cent. in the value of products.

INDUSTRIAL ESTABLISHMENTS

The number of Industrial Establishments in each County in 1891 (according to the census returns, the latest available figures) was as follows:—

Classification of Trade	King's	Prince	Queen's	Total
Aerated water making		1	2	3
Agricultural implements	1	9		10
Bakeries		2	6	8
Basket making		12		12
Blacksmithing	94	136	145	375
Boat building	5	8	10	23
Book-binding			3	3
Boots and Shoes	41	50	82	173
Breweries			1	1
Brick and Tile making	1	6	10	17
Forward	142	224	259	625

Classification of Trade	King's	Prince	Queen's	Total
Brought Forward	142	224	259	625
Cabinet and Furniture making	5	5	9	19
Carding and Fulling Mills	8	14	13	35
Carpenters and Joiners	78	82	116	276
Carpet making			25	25
Carriage making	17	43	32	92
Carriage Top making			1	1
Cheese Factories (now greatly increased)	1	2	1	4
Chemical Establishments			4	4
Confectionery			5	5
Cooperage	6	22	6	34
Dentistry		1	4	5
Dress Making and Millinery	24	36	104	164
Electric Light Works			2	2
Fish Canning (largely increased)	23	50	25	98
Fish curing	25	137	92	254
Fishing Tackle making		5	8	13
Flour and Grist Mills	23	42	47	112
Foundries and Machine Works	3	2	4	9
Gas Works			1	1
Harness and Saddlery	8	8	20	36
Hosiery Factories			2	2
Knitting Factories			3	3
Lath Mills		1		1
Lime Kilns	176	9	22	207
Lobster Trap making		9	1	10
Lobster Can and Box making			3	3
Marble and Stone cutting	3	1	3	7
Meat curing	8	5	14	27
Miscellaneous		1		1
Moss Factory			1	1
Painters and Glaziers	1	6	1	8
Patent Medicine Factories			1	1
Photographic Galleries		1	1	2
Picture Frame making			2	2
Planing and Moulding Mills	1	1		2
Plaster and Stucco Works		2		2
Plumbers and Gas Fitters			1	1
Potteries			1	1
Printing and Publishing Offices		2	4	6
Pump and Wind Mill Factories			3	3
Sail making	1	2	5	8
Forward	553	713	846	2112

Classification of Trade	King's	Prince	Queen's	Total
Brought Forward	553	713	846	2112
Sash, Door and Blind Factories	3	2	4	9
Saw Mills	51	66	55	172
Shingle making	5	11	16	32
Ship Yards	5	2	1	8
Shook and Fish Box making		1		1
Soap and Candle making			2	2
Spinning Wheel Factories		1		1
Starch Factories	3	1	2	6
Tailors and Clothiers	29	36	53	118
Tanneries	4	9	17	30
Tin and Sheet Iron Working	3		1	4
Tinsmithing	4	10	5	19
Tobacco Working			2	2
Trunk, Box and Valise making			3	3
Watchmakers and Jewellers		4	6	10
Weavers	60	33	45	138
Wood Turning	3	2		5
Woolen Mills	1	2	4	7
Totals	724	893	1062	2679

A census at the present time would probably show an increase in most of the above industries.

ATTRACTIONS FOR THE TOURIST AND SPORTSMAN

THIS lovely Island possesses immense attractions for tourists and there is no better summer resort in all America. It is an outing paradise, and a wonder to those who visit it for the first time. Instead of the doubtful allurements of a conventional seaside resort, there will be found the finest surf-bathing in the world, excellent fishing and game in season. A number of comfortable hotels and farm houses are open to the tourist at moderate rates, where the tired toilers of the hot and dusty cities can find health and enjoyment. There are many enticing places on both the north and south shores—

"With spots of sunny openings, and with nooks
To lie and read in, sloping into brooks."

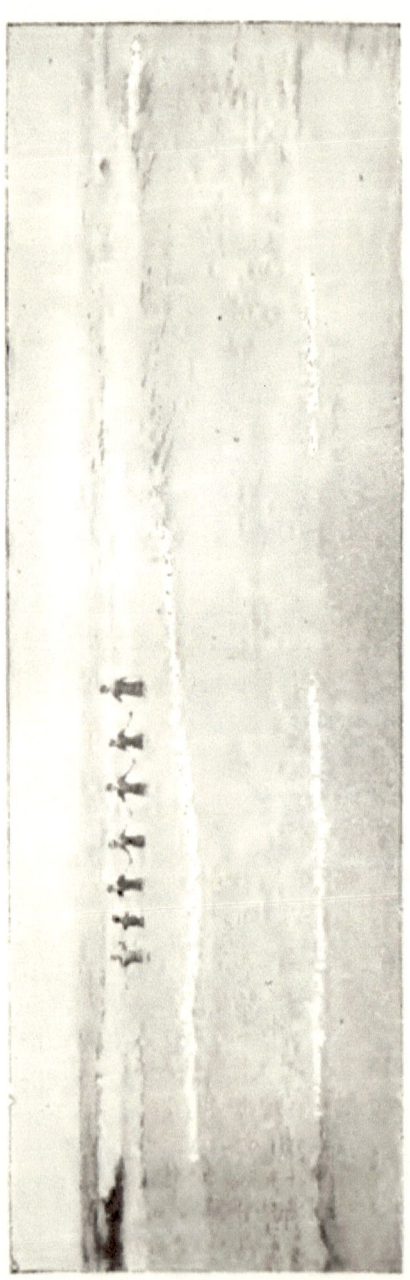

"THE FINEST SURF-BATHING IN THE WORLD"

Several Americans have erected cottages for their own use, and the number of tourists is yearly increasing. With more extensive advertising and greater hotel accomodation the summer – visitor "industry" would be a veritable mine to the country.

The best drinking water in the world, a wild and cultivated strawberry season extending from July 1st until late in August, with raspberries and other small fruit of an equally good quality closely following, pretty and quaint subjects for the camera at every turn, with the free use of "dark rooms" in Charlottetown, for the development of pictures (or the option of having the work performed at a trifling cost) are a few of the many minor attractions that prospective visitors might make a note of.

FISH AND GAME

There is no large game or extensive salmon fly-fishing; but sportsmen will find good shooting in the shape of wild geese, brant, duck, wood-cock, plover, and snipe during the season. By an Act of the Legislature, passed in 1898, the killing of partridge was prohibited for two years. The Morell, Midgell, Dunk, Pierre Jacques, Miminigash, Kildare, Tignish, Percival, Enmore, Winter River and other streams afford good trout fishing. There is also excellent fishing at North Lake and other places in the vicinity of East Point.

Fishing and Game Laws

The Dominion and Provincial Parliaments have passed laws to prevent the wanton destruction of fish and game, and for the establishment of close seasons.

The Dominion Trout-Fishing regulations are as follows :—

" In the Provinces of Nova Scotia, New Brunswick and Prince Edward Island, no one shall fish for, catch, kill, buy, sell or possess any speckled trout, salmon trout, gray trout, white trout, lake trout, winanish, toag, land-locked salmon, or any other kind of trout from the 1st day of October to the 31st day of March in each year, both days inclusive."

There are no other Government restrictions, but on some streams parties hold fishing leases. Further information can be obtained from the resident Fishery Officers.

Game Protection

An Act passed by the Provincial Legislature in 1879 for the protection of game and fur-bearing animals, together with an amendment in 1898, provides as follows :—

" None of the birds or animals hereinafter mentioned shall be taken or killed, or attempted to be taken or killed within the periods hereinafter mentioned : 1. Partridge between the 15th day of February and the 1st day of October. 2. Wood-cock and Snipe between the 1st day of January and the 20th day of August. 3. Water fowl which are known as wild duck between the 1st day of March and the 10th day of September. 4. Hares or rabbits between the 1st day of March and the 1st day of September. 5. Muskrat, martin or otter between the 1st day of May and the 1st day of November." The same shall not be had in possession or offered for sale during the periods in which they are so protected. No eggs shall be had in possession nor shall wood-cock be killed before sunrise or after sunset. The penalty for breaches of the Act is a fine not exceeding $25 nor less than $5 for each bird, animal or egg.

An Act to protect wild fowl, passed in 1884, prohibits the killing of any kind of wild fowl between sunset and sunrise, and the penalty for infractions of the same is $50.

PRINCE EDWARD ISLAND'S FUTURE
Agriculturally

WHILE the vigorous prosecution of the Fisheries, and Improved Winter Communication will be important factors in the welfare of this Province, upon the development of Agriculture more than anything else depends the Island's future prosperity. Farmers are throwing off their lethargy, and are adopting new ideas and methods. In the line of handling milk, growing fodder and caring for stock, wonderful advances have been made. The Dairy Industry is yielding a large revenue, and fruit-growing receiving more attention, is becoming remunerative.

An increased product in Pork is also a certainty. Charlottetown now possesses a modern pork-packing factory thoroughly equipped for the scientific slaughter of swine and the preparation of pork and its by-products. This will bring about new methods in the fattening of pigs, and scrub animals will become extinct.

But, nothwithstanding the great progress of recent years, specialties in the farming line are still in their infancy. Much ground is yet to be covered in both dairying and fruit-growing, whilst poultry-fattening is practically untouched.

With the opening up of the British Market to Island products, with the promised illustration and poultry-fattening station, realized, and with continued inspiration and assistance from the Dominion dairying and horticultural experts, agriculture in all its branches must rapidly advance, and concurrently with such progress, will the "Garden Province" enter upon an era of prosperity unprecedented in its history.

As a Field for the Farmer Emigrant

Although Prince Edward Island cannot expect many new settlers, since there is now comparatively little room for such, yet it is a desirable place for a certain class of immigrants in search of improved farms with buildings, and within easy reach of the social comforts of life. Good farms of this kind, some of which are vacated by those who turn their faces to the "Golden West," can from time to time be had at from $20 to $35 per acre.

Improved Winter Communication

The problem of continuous winter communication has not yet been solved, and the Winter Ferry and Georgetown-Pictou Routes are still uncertain. In the distant future, communication may possibly be had the year round by tunnel or subway (as was advocated some years ago), or perchance by balloon which may be one of the possibilities of the twentieth century; but in the meantime, the new winter steamer "Minto," that is expected to begin its work in the season of 1899-1900, will greatly improve the existing state of affairs.

As a Summer Resort

The spot that was described in the latter part of the last century by a prejudiced English writer (William Cobbett) as "a rascally heap of sand, rock and swamp, occupied only as a military station, and producing nothing but potatoes," is now designated a great garden, and is admitted by those who are fortunate enough to visit it, to be unexcelled as an outing-place in summer. A beauty that is unique has drawn many to its shores, but its strong attractions still remain comparatively unknown. What Tourists' Associations and first-class hotels have done and are doing for other places, that would they accomplish for this Province were its people and capitalists alive to their own interests.

To-day, the Island of Prince Edward which Cartier declared "the fairest that may possibly be seene," still delights. To the natural charm has long since been added that brought by cultivation. Set in the midst of the silver sea, with its wealth of verdure and smiling fields, the Island presents a sub-tropical appearance. The air redolent of the fragrance of grasses and flowers, the shining waters, and all the dreaminess of a Lotus-land, invite the tourist. Its hospitable people are ready to welcome increasing numbers of visitors. The great hotel must come, and with the good work of introducing modern ideas and improvements continued, the prosperity of this Ocean Garden Island is assured.

"UNEXCELLED AS AN OUTING-PLACE IN SUMMER"

THE principal "North Shore" Resorts are at Tracadie Beach, Stanhope Brackley Beach, Rustico, and Malpeque. At these places, respectively, are located the "Acadia," "Shaw's," the "Sea View," "Mutch's," the "Cliff House," the "Seaside," and the "North Shore" Hotels. These houses are delightfully situated on beautiful land-locked Bays, where boating, still-water bathing, shooting, and other sports may be enjoyed ad libitum. Beyond the bars and the sand dunes, rolls in the foam-capped surf, and here is the finest sea-bathing in America; while out in the Gulf, for those who fancy it, can be had mackerel and cod fishing with the hardy toilers of the North Bay. The strong air of this northern coast is a tonic in itself. The hotels are within easy drive of Charlottetown or other railway station. The "Seaforth" is at Cascumpec Bay.

But to those who prefer a less ozonized atmosphere, the "South Shore" offers many attractions. The "Florida" hotel is a popular resort at Pownal, and the "Lansdowne" at Cape Traverse is a comfortable house. The "Pleasant View" house at Hampton is very much liked by all who visit it. There is good boating and bathing, and the hotel is beautifully situated on high ground with an extensive and pretty view of land and sea. This place is reached by boat or carriage from Charlottetown.

Besides the hotels (a list of which follows), there are many farm houses where visitors will be welcomed and hospitably entertained. Numerous clean and intelligent families will receive tourists; and if the bill of fare be not as varied as that of the hotels, the guests may depend upon getting the richest cream and the most golden butter imaginable, together with an abundance of all the other good things furnished by this fertile summer-land.

"ROLLS IN THE FOAM-CAPPED SURF"

The following Hotels open for the season between June 15th and July 1st, closing early in September :—

On the North Shore

Place	Name	Proprietor	No. Acc.	Terms Per Day	Terms Per Week
Tracadie Beach	Acadia	I. C. Hall	100	2 50	8.00
Stanhope	Mutch's	F. Mutch	25	1.30	5-7.00
"	Cliff	J. J. Davies	40	*	
Brackley Beach	Shaw's	Neil Shaw	50	1.30	6-8 00
"	Sea View	E. Houston	40	1.00	5-6.00
Rustico	Seaside	J. Newson & Co.	70	1 75	7-10.00
Malpeque	North Shore	G. F. Bearisto	25	1.00	6-up
Alberton	Seaforth	G. R. Montgomery	20	1.50	7.00

On the South Shore

Place	Name	Proprietor	No. Acc.	Terms Per Day	Terms Per Week
Pownal	Florida	W. Brown	15	1 00	5-8.0 0
Hampton	Pleasant View	Matthew Smith	50	1.00	†5.00

List of Hotels

Name	Location	No. Acc'd	Terms Per Day	Terms Per Week
Davies	Charlottetown	150	$2 00 up	$10 50 up
Queen	"	80	1 50	6 00 up
Revere	"	60	1 00-1 50	4 00-7.00
Eureka	"	20	1 50-2 00	7 00
McMillan	Hunter River	10	1 00	4.00
Lansdowne	Cape Traverse	50	1 00 up	4.00-8.00
Clark's	Kensington	20	1 25	6 00
Commercial	"	20	1 00	5 00
Clifton	Summerside	40	2 00	Agt.
Russ	"	50	1.50	7.00
Campbell	"	40	1 25 up	6 00
Barclay	O'Leary	10	1 25	5.00
Albion Terrace	Alberton	40	1 50	5.00
Revere	"	20	1 00	1 00
Wisner	"	10	1 50	5 00
Railway	Tignish	10	1 00	5 00
Clark's	Mt. Stewart	10	1 00	4 00
Manson	"	10	1 00	4 00
Smith	Cardigan	10	1 25	5.00
McDonald	Montague		1.00-1 50	6 00
Aitken	Georgetown	20	1.50	Agt.
Tapper	"	10	1 50	5 00-6 00
Revere	"	15	1 00	3 00-5 00
Central	"	10	1 00	3 00-5.00
Dingwell	Morell			
McLean	St. Peter's	10	1 25	5 00
Fraser	"	10	1 25	5 00
Sea View	Souris	40	1 50	Agt.
Frederick	"	25	1 00	5 00

* Apply to the "Hotel Davies."
† $3 to family parties.

"WITH THE HARDY TOILERS OF THE NORTH BAY"

ROUTES, ETC.

Prince Edward Island is reached by boats of the " Plant Line " from Boston to Charlottetown (owing to the increased tourist traffic this season, the magnificent " La Grande Duchesse " being required in addition to the " Halifax,") and by direct steamers from Montreal ; by rail from Boston, St. John and Montreal to Point du Chene, N. B., thence by boat to Summerside, P. E. I.; by boat Boston to Yarmouth, thence rail to Pictou, N. S., and steamer to Charlottetown ; by rail from Halifax to Pictou, thence by boat to Charlottetown ; and from Halifax by direct steamer. The Tourists' Information Bureau at Charlottetown, and the Prince Edward Island Railway folders afford more specific information as to resorts, routes, etc. Copies of this pamphlet may be obtained from the Provincial Government, Charlottetown.

ADDENDA

Since the foregoing pages have been put into print, a change has taken place in the establishment of the Militia of this Province, referred to on page 21. The force is now composed of four companies of Garrison Artillery, with the strength of each company increased by 12 and a total establishment of 244, one double company of Engineers, and eight companies of Infantry, a total of 57 officers and 717 non-commissioned officers and men.

The direct steamship service to Great Britain, alluded to on pages 49 and 63, is to be continued. One of the boats of the Elder-Dempster Line, the " Lake Huron," will make several trips between Charlottetown and Liverpool this season.

Poultry-fattening stations (adverted to at page 71) have been established by the Dominion Government at Charlottetown and Summerside.

ERRATA

On page 20, top line, " Lib.-Con " should read " Lib."
On page 61, 15th line, omit the word " open."

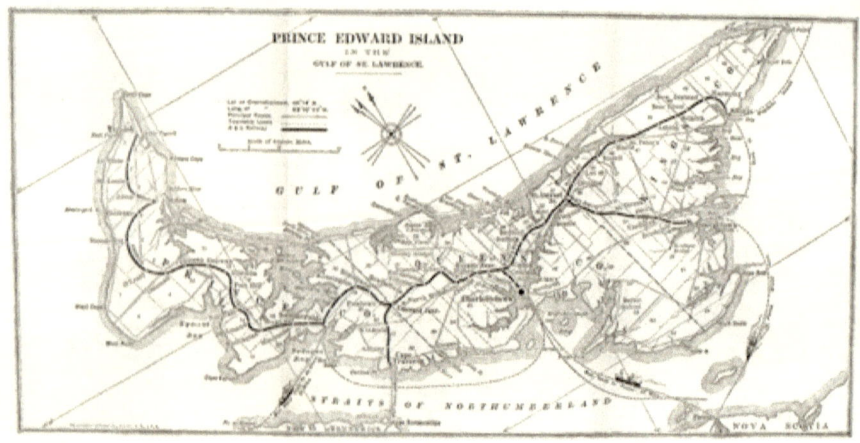

www.ingramcontent.com/pod-product-compliance
Lightning Source LLC
Chambersburg PA
CBHW022013050726
47499CB00007BA/2557